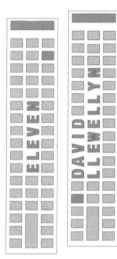

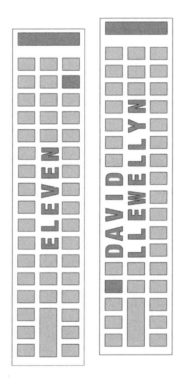

ELEVEN

DAVID LLEWELLYN

seren

Seren is the book imprint of
Poetry Wales Press Ltd
57 Nolton Street, Bridgend, CF31 3AE, Wales
www.seren-books.com

ISBN 1-85411-415-8

A CIP record for this title is available from
the British Library.

The publisher works with the financial assistance of the
Welsh Books Council.

Printed in Arial by CPD (Wales), Ebbw Vale

To Dad and Andrew

and in memory of my Mum,

Elizabeth Llewellyn

FROM: martin.davies@quantumfinance.co.uk
TO:
SAVED: 08:33, Tuesday September 11, 2001
SUBJECT: F**king Tuesdays

Last night we went for a drink on Mill Lane. You should have come.

Anyway, as it was starting to get dark this guy came up to us, a crazy guy with a beard and he said "take all your money out of your bank accounts, spend all your credit cards, the revolution will not be televised".

He kept saying it was going to be the end of the world, so we might as well spend everything we've got.

Then I realised that I've already spent everything that I've got. My credit cards and store cards are already maxed, so I'm fucked.

I couldn't sleep when I got

SAVED IN 'DRAFTS'

FROM: martin.davies@quantumfinance.co.uk
TO:
SAVED: 08:39, Tuesday September 11, 2001
SUBJECT: Morning!

I just started writing you an email, and then I realised that it was too boring for words, so I'm writing this one instead.

How are you today?

You should have come out with us last night. Went to Mill Lane. It was kind of fun. Distracting, really, more than fun. Lisa got into an argument with the guy in Dorothy's saying he short-changed her.

Couldn't sleep when I got in. I think I woke up about

four times. Kept having these really horrible dreams about my job. I had one dream in which Sue, my manager, took me out into the middle of this great big lake, and told me that if I wanted to get my promotion I would have to spear three very large fish with a trident. So she gave me this trident, and she pointed to a place even further out into the lake. She said, "That's where you'll find the fish".

I started plunging the trident into the water, and I thought I had caught a fish, only when I lifted it out there was a baby on the end of the

SAVED IN 'DRAFTS'

✉

FROM: martin.davies@quantumfinance.co.uk
TO:
SAVED: 08:44, Tuesday September 11, 2001
SUBJECT: Morning!!

Hi. How are you? Mill Lane was fun last night. You should have come. Lisa got into a fight with the man in Dorothy's over her change and some crazy guy told us the world was going to end. Then I had a dream where I skewered a baby
FUCK IT FUCK IT FUCK IT FUCK IT

SAVED IN 'DRAFTS'

✉

FROM: Martin Davies
(mailto: martin.davies@quantumfinance.co.uk)
TO: lloydt@callotech.co.uk
SENT: 08:51, Tuesday September 11, 2001
SUBJECT: Morning!!!

How are you? Missed a good one last night. Lisa almost got into a fight over a tray of curry and chips, and some crazy bloke told us the world was going to end.

✉

FROM: Lloyd Thomas
(mailto: lloydt@callotech.co.uk)
TO: martin.davies@quantumfinance.co.uk
SENT: 08:55, Tuesday September 11, 2001
SUBJECT: RE: Morning!!!

The world is full of idiots and psychopaths, Martin my friend. This I have learned. And everyone drives like it's a Sunday the minute the kids r back in skool. F**kwits.
    Is there a really cute black bird on your department? Well, not black, really. Half-caste, or mixed race, or whatever you say now. Really pretty. Long grey coat. What's her name?

✉

FROM: Martin Davies
(mailto: martin.davies@quantumfinance.co.uk)
TO: lloydt@callotech.co.uk
SENT: 08:58, Tuesday September 11, 2001
SUBJECT: What?

Idiots and psychopaths. What makes us different?

As for the mixed race girl (as I believe the preferred term would be), Lloyd… There are 1500 people in this building, on three different floors. I don't have a f**king clue who you are on about.

⊠

FROM: Corporate Communications
TO: All subjects
SENT: 08:59, Tuesday September 11, 2001
SUBJECT: Christmas Rota

Please be aware that a preliminary version of the Christmas Rota for Process Accounting is now available on the intranet under human resources/business maintenance/rota/rota-dec. If you have any queries regarding shifts, please forward them to Philip Greenwood in Human Resources.

⊠

FROM: Martin Davies
TO: Safina Aziz
SENT: 09:01, Tuesday September 11, 2001
SUBJECT: Christmas! Bah humbug

Have you seen the Christmas Rota?

⊠

FROM: Safina Aziz
TO: Martin Davies
SENT: 09:02, Tuesday September 11, 2001
SUBJECT: RE: Christmas! Bah humbug

I know. Takes the pi$$, doesn't it? What are you working?

⊠

FROM: Martin Davies
TO: Safina Aziz
SENT: 09:02, Tuesday September 11, 2001
SUBJECT: RE: RE: Christmas! Bah humbug

Everything. Christmas Eve. Boxing Day. I'm off New Year's Eve but back in New Year's Day. How about you?

⊠

FROM: Safina Aziz
TO: Martin Davies
SENT: 09:03, Tuesday September 11, 2001
SUBJECT: RE: RE: RE: Christmas! Bah humbug

Off Christmas Eve. In everything else. They're such f*king ba$tards.

✉

FROM: Martin Davies
TO: Safina Aziz
SENT: 09:03, Tuesday September 11, 2001
SUBJECT: RE: RE: RE: RE: Christmas! Bah
               humbug

Don't you mean "f**king"? There are two *s in f**king.

✉

FROM: Safina Aziz
TO: Martin Davies
SENT: 09:03, Tuesday September 11, 2001
SUBJECT: Very funny

Ha ha ha. Very funny.

✉

FROM: Lloyd Thomas
(mailto: lloydt@callotech.co.uk)
TO: martin.davies@quantumfinance.co.uk
SENT: 09:03, Tuesday September 11, 2001
SUBJECT: What we need is cameras

I've told you before, you need to get surveillance on these laydeez, Mr Davies. Otherwise you are going to end up single for the rest of your days. Are you sat near that paki girl today?

⊠

FROM: Martin Davies
(mailto: martin.davies@quantumfinance.co.uk)
TO: lloydt@callotech.co.uk
SENT: 09:05, Tuesday September 11, 2001
SUBJECT: Political Correctness?

If you mean Saffy, no I'm not sat near her. She's training on another bank of desks today. And anyway, what's it got to do with you, my politically insensitive friend?

⊠

FROM: Lloyd Thomas
(mailto: lloydt@callotech.co.uk)
TO: martin.davies@quantumfinance.co.uk
SENT: 09:05, Tuesday September 11, 2001
SUBJECT: RE: Political Correctness?

Yes, I did mean Saffy. And as for what has it got to do with me, I'm merely taking an interest in your love life, young man. This is all part of your rehabilitation.

⊠

FROM: Martin Davies
(mailto: martin.davies@quantumfinance.co.uk)
TO: lloydt@callotech.co.uk
SENT: 09:06, Tuesday September 11, 2001
SUBJECT: RE: RE: Political Correctness?

My rehabilitation? What do you mean by that? There's nothing to rehabilitate. I'm rehabilitated already. I never needed rehabilitating in the first f**king place.

✉

FROM: Lloyd Thomas
(mailto: lloydt@callotech.co.uk)
TO: martin.davies@quantumfinance.co.uk
SENT: 09:06, Tuesday September 11, 2001
SUBJECT: Whoa whoa whoa

Easy tiger. No offence intended. It's just you've been single a while now, and I know you've been out of the house and everything, but we need to get you back on the tracks and back in the ball park, hitting the wide shots, swinging the aces.

✉

FROM: Martin Davies
(mailto: martin.davies@quantumfinance.co.uk)
TO: lloydt@callotech.co.uk
SENT: 09:07, Tuesday September 11, 2001
SUBJECT: RE: Whoa whoa whoa

You don't half talk some $hit sometimes.

✉

FROM: Martin Davies
TO: Philip Greenwood
SENT: 09:09, Tuesday September 11, 2001
SUBJECT: Christmas Rota

Philip

I've just noticed that I'm down to work Christmas Eve, Boxing Day and New Year's Day over Christmas. I was just wondering whether this might get swapped around – my family don't live in Cardiff and it's hard getting back and fore to them on Bank Holidays. I can work extra shifts in the New Year, or between now and then. Appreciations in advance.

Regards, Martin

✉

FROM: Safina Aziz
TO: Martin Davies
SENT: 09:10, Tuesday September 11, 2001
SUBJECT: Cerys

I'm sorry, but have u seen what she's wearing? She looks like a tube of refreshers.

✉

FROM: Martin Davies
TO: Safina Aziz
SENT: 09:11, Tuesday September 11, 2001
SUBJECT: RE: Cerys

A tube? How about a f**king barrel? Horizontal stripes are not her friend.

✉

FROM: Safina Aziz
TO: Martin Davies
SENT: 09:11, Tuesday September 11, 2001
SUBJECT: RE: RE: Cerys

LMAO. That is SUCH a gay thing to say, but so true!

⊠

FROM: Martin Davies
TO: Safina Aziz
SENT: 09:13, Tuesday September 11, 2001
SUBJECT: RE: RE: RE: Cerys

What's a gay thing to say? The thing about the stripes? Why is that gay? I've got gay friends, so I've probably heard one of them, Lloyd's flatmates or somebody, say something like that. Or Will and Grace. I watch that sometimes. I'm not gay.

⊠

FROM: Safina Aziz
TO: Martin Davies
SENT: 09:13, Tuesday September 11, 2001
SUBJECT: RE: RE: RE: RE: Cerys

Chill, Winston. It's just you. You're funny.

⊠

FROM: martin.davies@quantumfinance.co.uk
TO:
SAVED: 09:14, Tuesday September 11, 2001
SUBJECT: I'm quitting

Sue

I know this is not enough notice, but I have decided to leave the company. I will not be coming back here tomorrow morning, as I feel it is time to move on to pastures new and
Fuckfuckfuckfuckfuckfuckfudjkflas;dfdljkgfal

SAVED IN 'DRAFTS'

⊠

FROM: Philip Greenwood
TO: Martin Davies
SENT: 09:20, Tuesday September 11, 2001
SUBJECT: RE: Christmas Rota

Hi Martin

Sorry, but the Rota is pretty much fixed at this moment in time.

Regards

Phil
Philip Greenwood, Senior Human Resources Manager
Email: philip.greenwood@quantumfinance.co.uk
Mob: 07975 555191
Tel: 02920 637801

⊠

FROM: martin.davies@quantumfinance.co.uk
TO:
SAVED: 09:20, Tuesday September 11, 2001
SUBJECT: RE: RE: Christmas Rota

You bald cunt. I suppose you'll be spending Christmas with your kids this year. Well I hope you choke on the fucking turkey you fat fuck. I hope the fucking tree catches fire and burns your fucking kids

SAVED IN 'DRAFTS'

⊠

FROM: Darren Andrews
TO: Martin Davies
SENT: 09:25, Tuesday September 11, 2001
SUBJECT: Jo!

Have you seen Jo's skirt? Like two apples in a hanky, oh yes!

⊠

FROM: Lloyd Thomas
(mailto: lloydt@callotech.co.uk)
TO: martin.davies@quantumfinance.co.uk
SENT: 09:29, Tuesday September 11, 2001
SUBJECT: The laydeez

So I showed a photo of you at the barbecue to Kelly, this girl in our office, and she's all like, 'whose your cute friend', and I'm all like, 'that's martin, he's single', and she's all like, 'when do I get to meet him then'.

You have got to take me up on this one, martin my friend. This girl is da bomb. She got tatties like you would not belieeeeve, and I'm telling you, when you see her batty waving around in front of you, you gonna whip that batty into shape, lemmee tell you.

⊠

FROM: Martin Davies
(mailto: martin.davies@quantumfinance.co.uk)
TO: lloydt@callotech.co.uk
SENT: 09:31, Tuesday September 11, 2001
SUBJECT: RE: The laydeez

Please don't email me in that bizarre Jamaican patois, or whatever it's meant to be, again. I'm not interested. Big tatties or no big tatties.

⊠

FROM: Lloyd Thomas
(mailto: lloydt@callotech.co.uk)
TO: martin.davies@quantumfinance.co.uk
SENT: 09:32, Tuesday September 11, 2001
SUBJECT: RE: RE: The laydeez

Saffy and Martin, sitting in a tree, F-U-C-K-I-N-G.

⊠

FROM: Martin Davies
(mailto: martin.davies@quantumfinance.co.uk)
TO: lloydt@callotech.co.uk
SENT: 09:33, Tuesday September 11, 2001
SUBJECT: RE: RE: RE: The laydeez

I am not seeing Saffy. I'm not even interested in her. She's my friend.

✉

FROM: Lloyd Thomas
(mailto: lloydt@callotech.co.uk)
TO: martin.davies@quantumfinance.co.uk
SENT: 09:34, Tuesday September 11, 2001
SUBJECT: RE: RE: RE: RE: The laydeez

And if she wasn't getting married?

✉

FROM: Susan Meredith
TO: Andrews, Darren; Aziz, Safina; Charles, Katherine; Davies, Martin; Gough, Lisa; Robinson, Suzie; Williamson, Joanne
SENT: 09:36, Tuesday September 11, 2001
SUBJECT: Appraisals

Here are the times for your September appraisals. Sorry they're late, but as you know I've been totally snowed under with the auditing for Cheltenham.

Friday Sept 14th –
Darren -   10am
Katie   -   11am
Martin   -   12pm

Saturday Sept 15th –
Jo   -   10am
Saffy   -   11am

Monday Sept 17th –
Lisa   -   1pm
Suzie   -   3pm

⊠

FROM: martin.davies@quantumfinance.co.uk
TO:
SAVED: 09:37, Tuesday September 11, 2001
SUBJECT: RE: Appraisals

Sue

This morning, on my way in to work, I saw a human turd under the bridge. I know it was a human turd because there was tissue paper next to it. Last Wednesday, on my way home from work, a prostitute on the corner of Trade Street asked me if I was looking for business.

Her face was dead, all smudged mascara and chipped teeth. Sometimes my head hurts just from looking at this stuff

SAVED IN 'DRAFTS'

⊠

FROM: Martin Davies
TO: Safina Aziz
SENT: 09:41, Tuesday September 11, 2001
SUBJECT: We gotta get out of this place if it's the last thing we ever do

I've got to get another job. I think I'm having some sort of breakdown. I can't do this any more. The phones are ringing and my head is full of noise.

✉

FROM: Gini Mayhew
TO: Business Maintenance Users
SENT: 09:44, Tuesday September 11, 2001
SUBJECT: Congratulations

Congratulations to Laura Berry from Process Accounting, who has given birth to a baby boy, Levi, 9lbs 6oz. Mother and baby are fine. Laura will not be coming back to work until December, but Debbie Phillips in accounts will be taking a collection for her. Anyone wishing to make a donation can contact Debbie on extension 6180.

✉

FROM: Safina Aziz
TO: Martin Davies
SENT: 09:47, Tuesday September 11, 2001
SUBJECT: RE: We gotta get out of this place if it's the last thing we ever do

I know. They're all w*nkers. I just had some guy on the phone trying to tell me that we over-charged him, and we didn't over-charge him. He's just being a dick.
Never mind. Three more weeks of this bull$hit and I'm on holiday.

⊠

FROM: Martin Davies
TO: Safina Aziz
SENT: 09:47, Tuesday September 11, 2001
SUBJECT: RE: RE: We gotta get out of this place if it's the last thing we ever do

Holiday?

⊠

FROM: Safina Aziz
TO: Martin Davies
SENT: 09:48, Tuesday September 11, 2001
SUBJECT: RE: RE: RE: We gotta get out of this place if it's the last thing we ever do

Honeymoon, stupid. Four weeks in Pakistan with my mad aunties. You should meet them – they are SO funny. My one aunty drives this Citroen 2CV, only she can't drive at all. She's had more crashes than you've had hot dinners. My other aunty can't speak much English, so if someone's big she just calls them fat. It's SO embarrassing. You should SO meet them.

✉

FROM: Martin Davies
TO: Safina Aziz
SENT: 09:49, Tuesday September 11, 2001
SUBJECT: RE: RE: RE: RE: We gotta get out of this place if it's the last thing we ever do

And they are SO on the other side of the planet, so I'm not going to.

✉

FROM: Lisa Cullis
(mailto: l.cullis@portersimpsonporter.co.uk)
TO: martin.davies@quantumfinance.co.uk
SENT: 09:53, Tuesday September 11, 2001
SUBJECT: Oh. My. God.

Hangover from Hell. It should be turned into a documentary and put on Channel Five.

Why does my head hurt, Martin. Why? Why?

I slept late this morning, and neither you nor Sara woke me. I had to buy breakfast in Greggs. GREGGS, Martin. Did you know they don't do croissants?

What the hell kind of a bakery doesn't do crois-sants? What year do they think it is….. 1930 or something? I had to have a "sausage and bean melt" for my breakfast. I still have no idea what that's meant to be. It did absolutely nothing to help the food poison-ing I contracted from my food last night. And why didn't you stop me from getting a takeaway? I was meant to be doing this f**king Atkins Diet that everyone's talking about. Curry and chips is hardly carb free. Next time we are out drinking do not let me go anywhere near Chippy Alley, no matter how much I beg or cry. I do not need chips, the chips need me.

Did I snog anyone in Ha Ha's last night? I had this funny smell in my nose this morning. Not unpleasant, but not very girly. I think it was Fahrenheit, but I'm not sure. Do you use Fahrenheit? Actually… What do you smell of? Martin Smell.

What's Martin Smell? And can I get a Magic Tree in it?

How are you this morning? I hope your head hurts as much as mine does. You seemed a bit quiet last night. Things okay? $hitty job getting you down? Still pining after that girl that Lloyd was on about last week? What's her name? Biffy?

Jiffy? Zippy? Bungle?

✉

FROM: Martin Davies
(mailto: martin.davies@quantumfinance.co.uk)
TO: l.cullis@portersimpsonporter.co.uk
SENT: 09:58, Tuesday September 11, 2001
SUBJECT: RE: Oh. My. God.

Your head hurts because you are dehydrated and your brain has shrunk. It's pulling on lots of microscopic fibres connecting it to the inside of your skull, which is causing painful tension. You don't have food poisoning, you have alcohol poisoning as a result of knocking back ten red After Shocks and seven pints of Stella last night...
   And her name is Saffy.

⊠

FROM: Lloyd Thomas
(mailto: lloydt@callotech.co.uk)
TO: martin.davies@quantumfinance.co.uk
SENT: 10:01, Tuesday September 11, 2001
SUBJECT: So....?

You didn't answer my f**king question, c*nt. What if she wasn't getting married?

⊠

FROM: Martin Davies
(mailto: martin.davies@quantumfinance.co.uk)
TO: lloydt@callotech.co.uk
SENT: 10:02, Tuesday September 11, 2001
SUBJECT: RE: So....?

I didn't answer it because it was a stupid question. She's my friend.

✉

FROM: Lloyd Thomas
(mailto: lloydt@callotech.co.uk)
TO: martin.davies@quantumfinance.co.uk
SENT: 10:02, Tuesday September 11, 2001
SUBJECT: RE: RE: So....?

Is it because she's of an Asian origin, because if it's because she's from an Asian origin, that makes you a racialist. Are you being a racialist, Martin? It's not nice being racialist at pakis.

✉

FROM: Martin Davies
TO: Susan Meredith
SENT: 10:02, Tuesday September 11, 2001
SUBJECT: Break

Can I grab a quick fag break?

✉

FROM: Susan Meredith
TO: Martin Davies
SENT: 10:03, Tuesday September 11, 2001
SUBJECT: RE: Break

Sure. As soon as Cerys comes back you can go for a break.

✉

FROM: martin.davies@quantumfinance.co.uk
TO:
SAVED: 10:15, Tuesday September 11, 2001
SUBJECT: Break

In the car park there are two fenced off spaces that have been allocated to the smokers and that's where we stand.

There's one guy who's always smiling. He's always on his own, and he's always smiling to himself, as if he's about to start laughing. I feel so nervous around people like that. I wonder was he always like that or has it happened since he started working here?

I'm beyond bored. Boredom would be comforting right now.

This is something else. This is everything.

SAVED IN 'DRAFTS'

✉

FROM: Lloyd Thomas
(mailto: lloydt@callotech.co.uk)
TO: martin.davies@quantumfinance.co.uk
SENT: 10:19, Tuesday September 11, 2001
SUBJECT: I'm sowwy

Have I upset you? Sorry if I have. You knows I'm only joshing, bra. Safe.

✉

FROM: Graham McKenzie
TO: Martin Davies
SENT: 10:21, Tuesday September 11, 2001
SUBJECT: Torcross Insulation

Martin,

I've just had a call from Terry Conway at Torcross Insulation in Plymouth concerning the proposal for Benningtons of Newton Abbot. I need to see if we can get this down to a flat rate of 4.5% otherwise it looks like we're going to lose the deal to GSB.

Regards

Graham

✉

FROM: Martin Davies
TO: Tony Cuccinello
SENT: 10:23, Tuesday September 11, 2001
SUBJECT: Fwd: Torcross Insulation

Tony

Would it be possible to get Torcross Insulation's flat rate down to 4.5%? Graham McKenzie would like to know.

Martin

✉

FROM: Tony Cuccinello
TO: Martin Davies
SENT: 10:24, Tuesday September 11, 2001
SUBJECT: RE: Fwd: Torcross Insulation

Martin

Sorry, but we've already given Torcross Insulation a flat rate of 5.2%, based on the success we've had with their clients in the past. Graham should be fully aware of this, as we discussed it back in July.

✉

FROM: Martin Davies
TO: Graham McKenzie
SENT: 10:25, Tuesday September 11, 2001
SUBJECT: Torcross Insulation

Graham

Sorry, but we are unable to offer anything less than 5.2% as a flat rate to Torcross Insulation. I've confirmed this with Tony Cuccinello.

Martin

⊠

FROM: Graham McKenzie
TO: Martin Davies
SENT: 10:26, Tuesday September 11, 2001
SUBJECT: RE: Torcross Insulation

Have another word with Tony for me would you? There's a lot of commission riding on this one, so they're breathing down my neck a bit, and we've really got to get our figures up for the South West, as they are trailing behind the South East and the North.

⊠

FROM: martin.davies@quantumfinance.co.uk
TO:
SAVED: 10:27, Tuesday September 11, 2001
SUBJECT: RE: RE: Torcross Insulation

You stupid, desperate cunt. When did you tear out your own soul and fill the empty space with nothing but monthly targets and expenses paid lunches? What are you angling for this quarter? A set of steak knives? A weekend for two to see some crappy Andrew Lloyd-Wanker show in the West End? Fuck you, Graham. Fuck you and all of your fucking kind.

SAVED IN 'DRAFTS'

✉

FROM: Lisa Cullis
(mailto: l.cullis@portersimpsonporter.co.uk)
TO: martin.davies@quantumfinance.co.uk
SENT: 10:30, Tuesday September 11, 2001
SUBJECT: RE: RE: Oh. My. God.

How wonderfully clinical of you. I do not have alcohol poisoning. I have drunk far more than I drank last night, and besides, would you trust anything you picked up from chippy alley? The place is probably crawling with e-coli. I just don't think its right having $ex shops and fast food places on the same street. Fisting and chips are not a good combination.

I had such a bollocking off Mark this morning. He was not impressed. My hair was like a mad woman's $hit when I came in, and none of my clothes were ironed. I think this means that you and Sara owe me a takeaway for not waking me up on time. Chinese will do, from the Happy Garden or whatever it's called. That one that does the nice crispy shredded beef, not the one that does the minging crispy shredded beef that looks like a brain.

Have you emailed that guy at the bbc yet about your script – the one Jessica was telling me about? His name is aneurin rhys-jones, so his email address is aneurin.rhys-jones@bbc.co.uk. You should definitely email him.

FROM:	Martin Davies
TO:	
SAVED:	10:33, Tuesday September 11, 2001
SUBJECT:	Scripts

Dear Aneurin

I am a twenty-six-year-old writer living in Cardiff, and have recently finished writing a screenplay. It is provisionally called 'The Meeting', and is about a policeman who

SAVED IN 'DRAFTS'

FROM: Corporate Communications
TO: All subjects
SENT: 10:35, Tuesday September 11, 2001
SUBJECT: Dress Down Charity

This month's dress-down day charity will be St Fagans Owl Sanctuary, nominated by Sheila Van Der Meer in Customer Services.

St Fagans Owl Sanctuary has been running since 1990. Over the past eleven years they have cared for over 170 owls from in and around the Cardiff area. They receive little government or lottery funding; the majority of their funds being raised from donations.
Collection boxes will be in the reception on Friday, Saturday and Sunday.

✉

FROM: Safina Aziz
TO: Martin Davies
SENT: 10:37, Tuesday September 11, 2001
SUBJECT: RE: RE: RE: RE: RE: We gotta get out of this place if it's the last thing we ever do

It's not like I'm moving there for good. It's just a honeymoon.

✉

FROM: Martin Davies
TO: Safina Aziz
SENT: 10:38, Tuesday September 11, 2001
SUBJECT: RE: RE: RE: RE: RE: RE: We gotta get
            out of this place, if it's the last thing we
            ever do

What?

⊠

FROM: Safina Aziz
TO: Martin Davies
SENT: 10:38, Tuesday September 11, 2001
SUBJECT: RE: RE: RE: RE: RE: RE: RE: We gotta
            get out of this place, if it's the last thing
            we ever do

You sounded a bit angry, that's all. I'm only going there
for a couple of weeks. Will you miss me?

⊠

FROM: martin.davies@quantumfinance.co.uk
TO:
SAVED: 10:40, Tuesday September 11, 2001
SUBJECT:

You don't want to marry him. We've had this conversa-
tion. He might be a decent man and all the rest of it, but
is it really what you

SAVED IN 'DRAFTS'

⊠

FROM: Dan Jones
(mailto: dan@mcpl-media.co.uk)
TO: martin.davies@quantumfinance.co.uk
SENT: 10:40, Tuesday September 11, 2001
SUBJECT: Howdy MD

Howdy MD,

Long time no hear. How's life in Cardiff? Sorry to hear about you and Theresa. When are you going to move to London? How many times do I have to tell you that Wales is fast becoming a nation of call-centre workers? Coalmines and coal ports have been replaced with great big air-conditioned graveyards of ambition. You would love it here, you'd be in your element. You are wasted in that $hitty admin job. I've got a friend who works for C4, says they're crying out for writers. Remember that thing you wrote when we were in college? Revenge of The P*rno Mutants, or whatever it was called… That was funny as f**k. Damn site funnier than most of the rubbish they're putting out at the moment. How many repeats of 'Friends' can you f**king watch?

Stacey and I have a theory – You can tell what series of 'Friends' you are watching by the size of Ross's hair, or the number of chins that Chandler has. Also… if it's really funny, it's probably series 2. If it's a bit lame and mawkishly sentimental, it's anything after series 2.

Come to London.

D'you hear that?

Come to London.

D. x

FROM: Martin Davies
(mailto: martin.davies@quantumfinance.co.uk)
TO: dan@mcpl-media.co.uk
SENT: 10:42, Tuesday September 11, 2001
SUBJECT: RE: Howdy MD

London means money, and I don't have any money. If I had money I'd move to London. As it is, I don't have any money, so I can't move to London. Besides, who ever believed all that Dick Whittington bull$hit?

✉

FROM: Dan Jones
(mailto: dan@mcpl-media.co.uk)
TO: martin.davies@quantumfinance.co.uk
SENT: 10:42, Tuesday September 11, 2001
SUBJECT: RE: RE: Howdy MD

Money schmoney. I moved here with about £500 and I've been living here six years. I'm earning £45k a year and I have a flat overlooking the Thames. I met Jeremy Irons last week. Jeremy f**king Irons.
    Move to London.

✉

FROM: martin.davies@quantumfinance.co.uk
TO:
SAVED: 10:44, Tuesday September 11, 2001
SUBJECT:

Dear Aneurin

I am a twenty-six-year-old writer living in Cardiff. I have
recently written a screenplay, provisionally titled 'The
Meeting'. It is about a policeman in Cardiff investigating
the grisly death of a teenage male prostitute, whose
body has been found on waste ground near the old
docks. His investigations lead him to a local celebrity
astrologer and mystic, thereby uncovering a

SAVED IN 'DRAFTS'

✉

FROM: Lloyd Thomas
(mailto: lloydt@callotech.co.uk)
TO: martin.davies@quantumfinance.co.uk
SENT: 10:45, Tuesday September 11, 2001
SUBJECT:

Has Lisa said anything about me?

✉

FROM: Martin Davies
(mailto: martin.davies@quantumfinance.co.uk)
TO: lloydt@callotech.co.uk
SENT: 10:46, Tuesday September 11, 2001
SUBJECT: RE:

What do you mean?

$$\boxtimes$$

FROM: Lloyd Thomas
(mailto: lloydt@callotech.co.uk)
TO: martin.davies@quantumfinance.co.uk
SENT: 10:46, Tuesday September 11, 2001
SUBJECT: RE: RE:

Nothing. It was just something that happened at the barbecue. I was wondering if she'd mentioned it.

$$\boxtimes$$

FROM: Martin Davies
(mailto: martin.davies@quantumfinance.co.uk)
TO: lloydt@callotech.co.uk
SENT: 10:47, Tuesday September 11, 2001
SUBJECT: RE: RE: RE:

No. Why?

$$\boxtimes$$

FROM: Lloyd Thomas
(mailto: lloydt@callotech.co.uk)
TO: martin.davies@quantumfinance.co.uk
SENT: 10:47, Tuesday September 11, 2001
SUBJECT: RE: RE: RE: RE:

Nothing. If she hasn't said anything then I probably shouldn't say anything.

$\boxtimes$

FROM: Martin Davies
(mailto: martin.davies@quantumfinance.co.uk)
TO: lloydt@callotech.co.uk
SENT: 10:48, Tuesday September 11, 2001
SUBJECT: RE: RE: RE: RE: RE:

What's with the cloak and dagger? Have you been texting her again, because like I said, maybe it was a bit much last time. She only split up with Casey in July and they were together 6 YEARS. She's all over the place now. Didn't I explain the categories to you?

$\boxtimes$

FROM: Lloyd Thomas
(mailto: lloydt@callotech.co.uk)
TO: martin.davies@quantumfinance.co.uk
SENT: 10:49, Tuesday September 11, 2001
SUBJECT: RE: RE: RE: RE: RE: RE:

The categories?

$\boxtimes$

FROM: Martin Davies
(mailto: martin.davies@quantum.finance.co.uk)
TO: lloydt@callotech.co.uk
SENT: 10:52, Tuesday September 11, 2001
SUBJECT: RE: RE: RE: RE: RE: RE: RE:

The three categories of being single.
CATEGORY 1 – You have never been in a serious relationship. You are young, fresh-faced and new to the world.
CATEGORY 2 – You have just come out of that serious relationship which you really thought was going to be 'the one'. You are all messed up with nowhere to go, unable to stop thinking about the ex, no matter how hard you try. It doesn't matter if you are the dumper or the dumpee. You're still going to be Category 2 for a while.
CATEGORY 3 – You've come out of the dark woods of Category 2. You are older, wiser, and ready to take on the world once more.

Category 1s and Category 3s are compatible with anyone. Category 1s and Category 1s make nice couples... Young love and all the rest of it. Likewise, Cat 3 and Cat 3s make good couples, because they've been through it all before, but this time they have experience on their side.

Category 2s just don't mix, not even with each other. They're always thinking about the ex.

Lisa is still Category 2.

✉

FROM: Lloyd Thomas
(mailto: lloydt@callotech.co.uk)
TO: martin.davies@quantumfinance.co.uk
SENT: 10:53, Tuesday September 11, 2001
SUBJECT: RE: RE: RE: RE: RE: RE: RE: RE:

So what does that make you?

✉

FROM: Corporate Communications
TO: All subjects
SENT: 10:55, Tuesday September 11, 2001
SUBJECT: Quantum House Air Conditioning

Due to an electrical fault overnight the air conditioning and heating systems were cut off.

The facilities department has looked into the problem and it has now been rectified.

The temperature of the building will correct itself within the next few hours.

Thank you for your cooperation.

✉

FROM: Graham McKenzie
TO: Martin Davies
SENT: 10:56, Tuesday September 11, 2001
SUBJECT: Torcross Insulation

Hi Martin

Have you had a word with Tony, only I've just had Terry Conway from Torcross on the phone again asking me whether we've had any joy. It's make-or-break time on this one, I'm afraid, and Torcross are a big account. We don't need to lose them.

⊠

FROM: martin.davies@quantumfinance.co.uk
TO:
SAVED: 10:56, Tuesday September 11, 2001
SUBJECT:

Fuck off.

SAVED IN 'DRAFTS'

⊠

FROM: martin.davies@quantumfinance.co.uk
TO:
SAVED: 10:57, Tuesday September 11, 2001
SUBJECT: Adios

Sue

We both know I'm not meant to be here. You have been my manager for 18mths now, and I like to think we've built up a certain rapport. You aren't a corporate monster like some of the others, you know this is all bull$hit, surely? I mean, to actually ENJOY this work, you'd have to be insane, right? Who in their right mind, as a child, ever said, "When I grow up I'd like to process accounts for a large multinational finance company"? How can anyone wake up each morning and think, "Yes! Today I'm going to go and do good finance! I'm going to process accounts better than they've ever been processed before"? It's not fucking normal.

I repeat: I am NOT meant to be here. There are other things I could be doing right now. Did you know I've written a film?

SAVED IN 'DRAFTS'

✉

FROM: Lloyd Thomas
(mailto: lloydt@callotech.co.uk)
TO: martin.davies@quantumfinance.co.uk
SENT: 10:57, Tuesday September 11, 2001
SUBJECT: So…?

So? You didn't answer my question. If Lisa's a category 2, which category are you?

✉

FROM: Lisa Cullis
(mailto: l.cullis@portersimpsonporter.co.uk)
TO: martin.davies@quantumfinance.co.uk
SENT: 10:58, Tuesday September 11, 2001
SUBJECT:

Has Lloyd said anything to you about the barbecue?

✉

FROM: Martin Davies
(mailto: martin.davies@quantumfinance.co.uk)
TO: l.cullis@portersimpsonporter.co.uk
SENT: 10:58, Tuesday September 11, 2001
SUBJECT: RE:

What happened at the barbecue?

⊠

FROM: Lisa Cullis
(mailto: l.cullis@portersimpsonporter.co.uk)
TO: martin.davies@quantumfinance.co.uk
SENT: 10:59, Tuesday September 11, 2001
SUBJECT: RE: RE:

Nothing. He didn't say anything?

⊠

FROM: Martin Davies
(mailto: martin.davies@quantumfinance.co.uk)
TO: l.cullis@portersimpsonporter.co.uk
SENT: 10:59, Tuesday September 11, 2001
SUBJECT: RE: RE: RE:

Why do you ask?

⊠

FROM: Susan Meredith
TO: Andrews, Darren; Aziz, Safina; Charles,
               Katherine; Davies, Martin; Gough, Lisa;
               Robinson, Suzie; Williamson, Joanne
SENT: 11:00, Tuesday September 11, 2001
SUBJECT: Lunches

Jo   -   12:00
Suzie   -   12:00
Lisa   -   12:30
Martin -   12:30
Katie   -   12:30
Saffy   -   13:00
Darren -   13:00

⊠

FROM: Safina Aziz
TO: Martin Davies
SENT: 11:01, Tuesday September 11, 2001
SUBJECT:

Are you okay? You've gone quiet?

⊠

FROM: Martin Davies
TO: Safina Aziz
SENT: 11:01, Tuesday September 11, 2001
SUBJECT: RE:

I'm fine. Just a bit busy at the mo.

⊠

FROM: Lloyd Thomas
(mailto: lloydt@callotech.co.uk)
TO: martin.davies@quantumfinance.co.uk
SENT: 11:02, Tuesday September 11, 2001
SUBJECT: I pity the fool!

mr-t_1jpg(16kb)

✉

FROM: Lisa Cullis
(mailto: l.cullis@portersimpsonporter.co.uk)
TO: martin.davies@quantumfinance.co.uk
SENT: 11:05, Tuesday September 11, 2001
SUBJECT: Stupid people

So this man is driving to his mother-in-law's house, and he hasn't been there in two months or something, and he crashes into a wall that didn't used to be there. The wall had been there for two months or so, it was over eight feet tall, and the crash occurred at one o'clock in the afternoon, otherwise known as "broad daylight".

This man (his name is actually Michael Jackson) is now trying to sue South Hams District Council for not putting up a sign warning him about the new wall.

Two questions:

Where the f**k is South Hams?

What the hell does this crazy f**kwit think he's playing at? He's written us a long letter (and by letter I mean epistle) asking us to represent him in the case of Michael Jackson vs. South Hams District Council. Because he drove into an eight foot brick wall at one o'clock in the afternoon.

I can't take this any more, Marty. I'm going slowly nuts. Is it me or is the world populated entirely with stupid people? Lots of them.

I blame TV.

I saw something the other day… It was an old trailer, with Cecil B. DeMille advertising his forthcoming production, The Ten Commandments. So Cecil's sat there, at this desk showing the audience photos, and he's saying, "This is a photo of Charlton Heston, and I think you'll be amazed by how much he looks like Michaelangelo's statue of Moses"… I mean, have you ever heard anything as STUPID in your entire f**king life? As though Michaelangelo's statue was based on the real Moses? As though Moses just walked straight into Michaelangelo's studio and POSED?

How many Americans ended up thinking that Michaelangelo and Moses were around at the same time?

"Well, uh, shucks… Moses… that musta been around the fifteenth century. And Jesus? Why, uh, didn't he help us beat the Nazis at Iwo Jima?"

✉

FROM: Martin Davies
(mailto: martin.davies@quantumfinance.co.uk)
TO: l.cullis@portersimpsonporter.co.uk
SENT: 11:10, Tuesday September 11, 2001
SUBJECT: RE: Stupid people

I think you're right, Lisa. Most of the information we've received in the last hundred years has come to us in the form of adverts. The history of the world is being rewritten by shampoo and toothpaste companies.

In answer to your questions:

South Hams is in Devon. Theresa is from Totnes, and that's in South Hams.

Re: "What does the crazy f**k think he's playing at?"

He's probably seen an advert for one of those accident claim companies and he thinks he's got a case. He's clearly insane, but then again, he's from Devon.

I have two questions of my own.

Are you serious when you say you think you're going nuts?

Is it right to feel weird talking about your ex in the present tense (eg: 'Theresa is from Totnes', rather than 'Theresa was from Totnes')?

✉

FROM: Lisa Cullis
(mailto: l.cullis@portersimpsonporter.co.uk)
TO: martin.davies@quantumfinance.co.uk
SENT: 11:12, Tuesday September 11, 2001
SUBJECT: RE: RE: Stupid people

In answer to your questions:

No. I've tried the whole being depressed thing. The doctor gave me tryptophan and fluoxetine, which is basically prozac. Then I found out that they don't mix well with alcohol, not even in a good way, so I stopped being depressed. Now I stick to vodka and gin and stumbling into the occasional bush with my mascara running down my face. It's much more dignified than having to talk about it with your GP.

In the given context, either is grammatically correct, I guess. But as for feeling wrong… I don't know, Marty. She's left you, she's not dead. Do you want her dead?

✉

FROM: Lisa Cullis
(mailto: l.cullis@portersimpsonporter.co.uk)
TO: martin.davies@quantumfinance.co.uk)
SENT: 11:12, Tuesday September 11, 2001
SUBJECT: RE: RE: Stupid people

I just realised, that last bit was a bit dark. Even for us. Scratch the bit about Theresa being dead, because then if Theresa did die, in an accident or something, I'd feel really really bad. So I guess either is fine, but it's probably best if you talk about her in the present tense, just to avoid any bad karma.

✉

FROM: Lisa Cullis
(mailto: l.cullis@portersimpsonporter.co.uk)
TO: martin.davies@quantumfinance.co.uk
SENT: 11:13, Tuesday September 11, 2001
SUBJECT: RE: RE: Stupid people

Am I talking crap? I just checked my Sent Items, and I've been waffling.

Jase gave me a quick line of coke in the toilets just now and I'm trying to do about sixteen different things at once, but I'm having lots more fun talking to you, although this isn't really talking. Am I allowed to say coke on email? F**k it. I might be talking about coca cola. YOU DON'T KNOW THAT MR EMAIL PERSON.

But talking about Coke, there's a L'America night at The Emporium on Saturday, and the last one was FAB, so Jase wanted to know if you wanted any for this weekend? And can you ask Lloyd for me?

✉

FROM: Martin Davies
(martin.davies@quantumfinance.co.uk)
TO: l.cullis@portersimpsonporter.co.uk
SENT: 11:14, Tuesday September 11, 2001
SUBJECT: RE: RE: RE: Stupid people

Why can't you ask him?

☒

FROM: Lisa Cullis
(l.cullis@portersimpsonporter.co.uk)
TO: martin.davies@quantumfinance.co.uk
SENT: 11:15, Tuesday September 11, 2001
SUBJECT: RE: RE: RE: RE: Stupid people

Because it's weird and I can't go into it. Just ask him if
he wants to come along and does he want a gram of
the you-know-what.

☒

FROM: martin.davies@quantumfinance.co.uk
TO:
SAVED: 11:16, Tuesday September 11, 2001
SUBJECT:

What the hell is going on? Is there some great big
fucking secret you're all keeping from me? Did Lloyd
fuck Theresa? I always thought he wanted to. There
isn't a part of his brain that stops him from doing those
kind of things. He's developed this brilliant coping
mechanism for situations like that... He apologises and
somehow wins you over with charm alone, and next

thing you know you're saying sorry to him for some semi-imagined slight from five years ago that he's reminded you of. And all the while there's this more recent, even more shitty thing that he's done, and he's never REALLY said sorry for it, because he didn't REALLY mean it when he said it. Who did he fuck? Theresa? You? Sara? He's met Saffy outside of work? Bumped into her in a club or something? They worked out they had a mutual friend in me, hit it off, and now she's fucking him behind her fiance's back?

I'm not quite there am I? In the pecking order, I mean. I'm somehow strangely absent from all the boardroom meetings you must have to discuss what we're doing as a group, because I don't ever seem to be there when the facts get found out or the decisions get made.

At what point did I become so fucking passive?

SAVED IN 'DRAFTS'

⊠

FROM: Martin Davies
(mailto: martin.davies@quantumfinance.co.uk)
TO: lloydt@callotech.co.uk
SENT: 11:17, Tuesday September 11, 2001
SUBJECT: The weekend

Lisa wants to know if you'd like a gram of you-know-what for the weekend.

⊠

FROM: Lloyd Thomas
(mailto: lloydt@callotech.co.uk)
TO: martin.davies@quantumfinance.co.uk
SENT: 11:17, Tuesday September 11, 2001
SUBJECT: RE: The weekend

It depends. If it's from Jase, probably not. The last stuff he got us didn't even feel like rubbish speed. I think it was crushed up aspirin and baby laxatives or something. If I'm going to abuse class A substances I want to come out in a cold sweat and have a numb face, not just sit there in my mate's living room asking everyone if they can feel anything yet. What else did Lisa say?

✉

FROM: Martin Davies
(mailto: martin.davies@quantumfinance.co.uk)
TO: lloydt@callotech.co.uk
SENT: 11:18, Tuesday September 11, 2001
SUBJECT: RE: RE: The weekend

Nothing.
    Now for the, like, tenth, and FINAL time, what the f**k happened between you and Lisa at the bar-b-q?

✉

FROM: Lloyd Thomas
(mailto: lloydt@callotech.co.uk)
TO: martin.davies@quantumfinance.co.uk
SENT: 11:18, Tuesday September 11, 2001
SUBJECT: RE: RE: RE: The weekend

As long as you and I are in offices on different sides of the city you can't give me a Chinese burn or threaten to destroy all my p0rn, so I'm not saying a word.

Furthermore, don't say "bar-b-q"… You're not an American-style diner in an out-of-town retail park.

Did you get the picture of Mr T?

✉

FROM: Martin Davies
(mailto: martin.davies@quantumfinance.co.uk)
TO: lloydt@callotech.co.uk
SENT: 11:19, Tuesday September 11, 2001
SUBJECT: RE: RE: RE: RE: The weekend

Yes, I got Mr T.

Thankyou.

✉

FROM: Lloyd Thomas
(mailto: lloydt@callotech.co.uk)
TO: martin.davies@quantumfinance.co.uk
SENT: 11:19, Tuesday September 11, 2001
SUBJECT: RE: RE: RE: RE: RE: The weekend

Isn't it awesome? And Phil, says he's got one some-where of the kid off Diff'rent Strokes posing with David Hasselhof in front of KIT… The only thing more 80s would be E.T. sinking the Belgrano, dressed as the guy out of Kajagoogoo.

I thought you could use it as wallpaper on your pc.

✉

FROM: Martin Davies
(mailto: martin.davies@quantumfinance.co.uk)
TO: lloydt@callotech.co.uk
SENT: 11:20, Tuesday September 11, 2001
SUBJECT: RE: RE: RE: RE: RE: RE: The weekend

No can do. They're kind of funny about us doing stuff like that. We can't personalise anything. We can't put up pictures. We can't customise our PCs. Everything has to look the same as everything else.

✉

FROM: Safina Aziz
TO: Martin Davies
SENT: 11:22, Tuesday September 11, 2001
SUBJECT: Wedding

I've given this some thought, and I've decided to ask you:
   Do you want to come to my wedding? I don't mind if you say no, because it's not going to be everyone's kind of thing – that's why I haven't asked anyone from work. I mean, Saida from hotline is going, but only because she's my Mum's best friend's sister. But I didn't know whether you might want to come? No booze, I'm afraid, and there won't be a karaoke!!!

✉

FROM: Lloyd Thomas
(mailto: lloydt@callotech.co.uk)
TO: martin.davies@quantumfinance.co.uk
SENT: 11:23, Tuesday September 11, 2001
SUBJECT: RE: RE: RE: RE: RE: RE: RE: The
             weekend

What? That sucks. Do you actually work for the f**king Victory company out of 1984 or something? Dude, get out of that job right now... Come do my job for me. My boss just called me a "f**king cretin", and though he was laughing I don't think he was joking. He was laughing, and kind of smiling, but his eyes had this homicidal intent behind them.
   I hate it when he does that.

✉

FROM: Lisa Cullis
(mailto: l.cullis@portersimpsonporter.co.uk)
TO: martin.davies@quantumfinance.co.uk
SENT: 11:25, Tuesday September 11, 2001
SUBJECT:

So does Lloyd want any or not, only Jase will be putting in his order for how much he needs some time this evening, so he can pick it up on Thursday. It all sounds very exciting, in a Pablo Escobar style. Did you want some? You haven't bought some for a while, and quite frankly, though I realise I do earn considerably more than you, I can't afford to support your burgeoning coke habit. Sorry, darling, you know I don't mean that. But the more we buy the better it will be.

FROM: Corporate Communications
TO: All subjects
SENT: 11:27, Tuesday September 11, 2001
SUBJECT: Christmas Party

We know it's early, but already the sound of sleigh-bells is in the air, which can mean only one thing!
    THAT'S RIGHT!
    Tickets for this year's Christmas Party will be going on sale on October 1st.
    This year you have voted for a party for the whole company, rather than individual department gatherings, to be held at Cardiff International Arena (the CIA), on Saturday, December 1st. Tickets will be £6 for staff and £36 for guests. The theme will be 'Christmas In Vegas'.
    IMPORTANT: Please remember that while the point

of a party is indeed to have fun, we cannot have a repeat performance of previous occasions, when a minority of people have overstepped the mark, and behaved in a way which brought the company into disrepute.

To avoid any embarrassment, unpleasantness or even (and we have to say it because it has happened) disciplinary action, please remember that when attending any Christmas functions run by, or subsidised by, the company we are still representing the company and the same rules apply.

SO LET'S NOT GET INTO ANY BOTHER OR BRING THE COMPANY INTO DISREPUTE THROUGH ERRANT BEHAVIOUR. LET'S HAVE A GREAT TIME OVER THE FESTIVE PERIOD.

✉

FROM: Safina Aziz
TO: Martin Davies
SENT: 11:30, Tuesday September 11, 2001
SUBJECT: Wedding

Hello?

✉

FROM: Graham McKenzie
TO: Tony Cuccinello
CC: Martin Davies; Susan Meredith
SENT: 11:33, Tuesday September 11, 2001
SUBJECT: Torcross Insulation

Hi, Tony,

Just to let you know, unfortunately we've had a spot of bother with Torcross Insulation this morning. They were setting up an account for Benningtons of Newton Abbot, and I asked Martin to check if we could get the flat rate down to 4.5% from 5.2%, or else we were going to lose the business to GSB. This wasn't done, and now Torcross are threatening to move all of their business to GSB in the future. Just thought you should be aware of the situation.

Graham

✉

FROM: Susan Meredith
TO: Martin Davies
SENT: 11:35, Tuesday September 11, 2001
SUBJECT: Torcross Insulation

Martin,

I've arranged a meeting for you and me with Tony later on this afternoon. I don't think he's too happy that you didn't tell him about GSB chasing after the competition. I'll let you know what time after lunch.

Sue

✉

FROM: Dan Jones
(mailto: dan@mcpl-media.co.uk)
TO: martin.davies@quantumfinance.co.uk
SENT: 11:40, Tuesday September 11, 2001
SUBJECT: Check this out

Ok, get this... We have just landed the contract to provide the multimedia for the opening of a new film and sound archive in Docklands, right? I'm heading the visuals team. Guess, my friend, who is hosting the opening?

Judy f**king Dench. That's right, my friend. M is hosting the opening, and I am going to be there, talking to her. Now... It's not happening until February. If I had an old friend from back home living in London some time around then, maybe I could manage to blag an invite for them too, and they could meet Judy f**king Dench, not to mention whoever else is going to be there. These things usually get weirdly famous people in – you know, so they can show off some intellectual credentials:

"Oh, it's not all awards ceremonies and GMTV dahling."

You know what I mean.

Move to London.

✉

FROM: Lloyd Thomas
(mailto: lloydt@callotech.co.uk)
TO: martin.davies@quantumfinance.co.uk
SENT: 11:43, Tuesday September 11, 2001
SUBJECT: FW: The funniest joke in the world?

In 1999, after years of research, British scientists identified what they called 'the funniest joke in the world'. Here it is:

A couple of New Jersey hunters are out in the woods

when one of them falls to the ground. He doesn't seem to be breathing; his eyes are rolled back in his head. The other guy whips out his cell phone and calls emergency services. He gasps to the operator, "My friend is dead! What can I do?" The operator, in a calm soothing voice says, "Just take it easy. I can help. First, let's make sure he's dead." There is silence. Then a gunshot is heard. The guy comes back on the line. "Okay," He says, "now what?"

✉

FROM: Safina Aziz
TO: Martin Davies
SENT: 11:54, Tuesday September 11, 2001
SUBJECT: Wedding

Did you get my email about the wedding? You've gone quiet.

✉

FROM: Lloyd Thomas
(mailto: lloydt@callotech.co.uk)
TO: martin.davies@quantumfinance.co.uk
SENT: 11:59, Tuesday September 11, 2001
SUBJECT: Quick question

I've been thinking about that documentary we saw the other night when you were round ours, about the equator, and the way that water spins round one way if you're north of it, and a different way if you're south of it, and it doesn't spin at all if you're right on the equator, it just goes down the plughole. Surely with the universe this rule will also apply.

So if our galaxy turns in one direction, then surely a galaxy somewhere must be turning in another direction, and somewhere there's a galaxy that's not spinning at all. It's just kind of hanging there. Would that be a black hole? If the world stopped turning would everything fly off? But if turning is what is making the gravity keeping us all here, why do all things that move in this way have things fly off? ie, if you stick some Sugar Puffs to a disco ball, and then spin the disco ball really fast, all the Sugar Puffs are going to fly off, not stick to the ball even more.

What point am I missing here?

PS: Lots more to write than this, but my manager just called me a f**king cretin for the second time today, and this time he kissed his teeth. You know, like a Jamaican.

✉

FROM: Lisa Cullis
(mailto: l.cullis@portersimpsonporter.co.uk)
TO: martin.davies@quantumfinance.co.uk
SENT: 12:03, Tuesday September 11, 2001
SUBJECT: Coke

I've told Jase to get you a gram. F**k Lloyd – He'll only end up snorting all his before he leaves his place and then blagging more off us, anyway, so we might as well just cut out the middle man. Besides – Nadine is coming out on Saturday. Remember my friend from when I went to Thailand? The mad one? Well she always buys in tonnes of the stuff, so it's not like we'll run out. You owe me £45 quid.

xx

✉

FROM: Safina Aziz
TO: Martin Davies
SENT: 12:07, Tuesday September 11, 2001
SUBJECT: Wedding

You don't have to come to the mosque, you can just
come to the party if you like. Like I said, no booze, but
some of my cousins drink, so maybe one of them will
sneak a few cans in!

✉

FROM: Lisa Cullis
(mailto: l.cullis@portersimpsonporter.co.uk)
TO: martin.davies@quantumfinance.co.uk
SENT: 12:11, Tuesday September 11, 2001
SUBJECT: Saturday night

Hope you don't mind, but I've told Nadine she can stay
at ours on Saturday. Get Lloyd to bring his housemates
out with us… What are their names? Nadine loves gay
guys. Proper little fag hag she is. She's been sick in the
toilets in Heaven more times that you've had hot
dinners.

✉

FROM: Lloyd Thomas
(mailto: lloydt@callotech.co.uk)
TO: martin.davies@quantumfinance.co.uk
SENT: 12:16, Tuesday September 11, 2001
SUBJECT: My quick question

Okay… Maybe that was a bit much, so just the one question really. Why do we stick to the earth if it spins?
   PS: Did you get the joke?
   I thought it was 5hit.

⊠

FROM: Dan Jones
(mailto: dan@mcpl-media.co.uk)
TO: martin.davies@quantumfinance.co.uk
SENT: 12:21, Tuesday September 11, 2001
SUBJECT: London, baby, London

So I can't even tempt you down here with the promise of Judi Dench?
   DAME Judi Dench.
   Oh come on, for the love of Christ! The woman is a god!

⊠

FROM: System Administrator
TO: Martin Davies
SENT: 12:25, Tuesday September 11, 2001
SUBJECT: Your mailbox is over its size limit

Your mailbox has exceeded one or more size limits set by your administrator.
   Your mailbox size is 41636 KB.

Mailbox size limits:

You will receive a warning when your mailbox reaches 40000 KB.

You may not be able to send or receive new mail until you reduce your mailbox size.

See client Help for more information.

⊠

FROM: Lloyd Thomas
(mailto: lloydt@callotech.co.uk)
TO: martin.davies@quantumfinance.co.uk
SENT: 12:28, Tuesday September 11, 2001
SUBJECT:

Okay then… simpler still… if things that turn make gravity, why don't we all get sucked into the Sun?

⊠

FROM: martin.davies@quantumfinance.co.uk
TO:
SAVED: 12:30, Tuesday September 11, 2001
SUBJECT:

Would you all just shut the fuck up?

SAVED IN 'DRAFTS'

⊠

FROM: Martin Davies
(mailto: martin.davies@quantumfinance.co.uk)
TO:
SENT:
SUBJECT:

I am out of the office until 13:30. Please forward queries
to accounts-processing@quantumfinance.co.uk

✉

FROM: martin.davies@quantumfinance.co.uk
TO:
SAVED: 13:29, Tuesday September 11, 2001
SUBJECT: Words

I don't know who I'm even writing this for. Half the time
I'm just looking at the reflection of my eyes in the
monitor. They look black. Why the fuck did I come back
here?

Half way through my lunch hour I fell asleep in one
of the toilet cubicles, with my trousers round my ankles
and my head against the toilet roll dispenser. I had one
of those dreams, those split-second dreams you get
when you aren't properly asleep, in which the toilet
cubicle was suddenly an elevator plunging down and
down into the ground. When I snapped to again I could
hear the sound of the person in the next cubicle pissing
and clearing his throat.

I work so that I can have money so that I can carry
on living in my house and I can eat. I do those things in
order that I can get up each day and go to work, and
maybe, in the days that fall between the times when I'm

working, I'll fill myself with chemicals and I'll put on a smile and pretend to be laughing. My pretend laugh is now more realistic than my real laugh. I do it even when somebody is telling me something really, really bad.

I work so I can live so I can work.

SAVED IN 'DRAFTS'

✉

FROM: Susan Meredith
TO: Martin Davies
SENT: 13:30, Tuesday September 11, 2001
SUBJECT: Meeting

Hi Martin

Tony is out of the office until five o'clock. I know you're finishing at five, and I hope you don't mind, but I've pencilled us in for a meeting then. It won't last more than five or ten minutes, and you can have the time back tomorrow on your lunch, or you can come in ten minutes later. Whichever is easiest.

Sue

✉

FROM: martin.davies@quantumfinance.co.uk
TO:
SAVED: 13:33, Tuesday September 11, 2001
SUBJECT: Dreams

Sue

Did I ever tell you the dream I had about us? It was a while ago, and if popular psychology is to be believed it doesn't mean a thing. I dreamt that we were in a hotel. I think it was meant to be in Amsterdam, but I'm not sure. We were sat at the bar in the hotel, and they served us burgers. You asked the chef what was in the burgers, because you were worried about Mad Cow Disease, and he told you it wasn't beef, it was horse. You spat out your burger, and ran away, disgusted. I followed you to your room, and that's when you started taking your clothes off and rubbing soap on your breasts.

    I don't think the dream is about sex. I think it's about intimacy. I mean, isn't that what we're all after, at the end of the day? Just an hour, a minute, five fucking seconds of something that means something with somebody? Sometimes I

SAVED IN 'DRAFTS'

✉

FROM: Dan Jones
(mailto: dan@mcpl-media.co.uk)
TO: martin.davies@quantumfinance.co.uk
SENT: 13:37, Tuesday September 11, 2001
SUBJECT: London London London London

I've just seen an advert for a flat in Lavender Hill. It's just down the road from the BAC, remember where we went to see that play? The one about the arm? Looks fantastic. Three bedroom. Open plan. Simon in work has been on about moving out of his current place (he lives with a mad Irish bint) and Stacey loves Lavender Hill. I reckon we could afford to keep the place for a month or two, give you time to get your $hit together.

FROM: Martin Davies
(mailto: martin.davies@quantumfinance.co.uk)
TO: dan@mcpl-media.co.uk
SENT: 13:39, Tuesday September 11, 2001
SUBJECT: RE: London London London London

You know I'd like nothing better than to leave this f**king place and come to London. Everywhere I go I see places I went to with Theresa and it's starting to kill me. But it's a pipe dream. I'm at the edge of a two grand overdraft. I've maxed three credit cards. I've got a staff loan which I've only half paid off, but if I ever left the company I'd have to pay it off in full.
    They've got me where they want me, Dan.
    I'm sorry.

FROM: Lloyd Thomas
(mailto: lloydt@callotech.co.uk)
TO: martin.davies@quantumfinance.co.uk
SENT: 13:40, Tuesday September 11, 2001
SUBJECT: Knight-strokes!

gary+david_1jpg(8kb)

✉

FROM: Lisa Cullis
(mailto: l.cullis@portersimpsonporter.co.uk)
TO: martin.davies@quantumfinance.co.uk
SENT: 13:44, Tuesday September 11, 2001
SUBJECT: Tw*tted

Oh my god, this is so funny, jase and I just wnet to ha ha's for our lunch and we were goinag to gets some food, but they told us there would be a 45min wiat, so we just got pis$ed instead and fnished off his coke. I am so f**kng wasted its untru.

✉

FROM: Corporate Communications
TO: All subjects
SENT: 13:45, Tuesday September 11, 2001
SUBJECT: Smoking areas

It has come to the attention of building supervisors that people are not putting out their cigarettes in the designated ashtrays in the smoking area. Please remember,

these ashtrays are there to be used. DO NOT put out cigarettes on the floor, as these then have to be cleaned up.
Thank you

⊠

FROM: martin.davies@quantumfinance.co.uk
TO:
SAVED: 13:46, Tuesday September 11, 2001
SUBJECT:

Oh god

⊠

FROM: Safina Aziz
To: Martin Davies
SENT: 13:55, Tuesday September 11, 2001
SUBJECT: Wedding?

You didn't get back to me about the wedding?

⊠

FROM: Martin Davies
TO: Safina Aziz
SENT: 13:56, Tuesday September 11, 2001
SUBJECT: RE: Wedding?

I'm thinking about it. Sorry, I'll make up my mind, honest.

⊠

FROM: Lloyd Thomas
(mailto: lloydt@callotech.co.uk)
TO: martin.davies@quantumfinance.co.uk
SENT: 13:58, Tuesday September 11, 2001
SUBJECT: Did you know…?

Did you know that barophobia is a fear of gravity?

How the f**k can you be scared of GRAVITY? I mean… I don't understand gravity, but I'm not f**king scared of it.

Not only that, but how many barophobics do you reckon there were before Isaac Newton came along?

✉

FROM: Martin Davies
(mailto: martin.davies@quantumfinance.co.uk)
TO: lloydt@callotech.co.uk
SENT: 14:00, Tuesday September 11, 2001
SUBJECT: RE: Did you know…?

Is there a fear of fear?

✉

FROM: Lloyd Thomas
(mailto: lloydt@callotech.co.uk)
TO: martin.davies@quantumfinance.co.uk
SENT: 14:04, Tuesday September 11, 2001
SUBJECT: RE: RE: Did you know…?

Just looked it up, and do you know what? There is. Phobophobia. The fear of fears.

There's also:
Tocophobia – A fear of childbirth.
Kakorraphiaphobia – A fear of failure.
Monophobia – A fear of being alone.
Maniaphobia – A fear of insanity.
Gametophobia – A fear of marriage.
Hypegiaphobia – A fear of responsibility.
Nosophobia – A fear of disease.
Katagelophobia – A fear of ridicule.
Thanatophobia – A fear of death.
See? There's one for everyone and everything, from the cradle to the grave.

$$\boxtimes$$

FROM: Martin Davies
(mailto: martin.davies@quantumfinance.co.uk)
TO: lloydt@callotech.co.uk
SENT: 14:05, Tuesday September 11, 2001
SUBJECT: RE: RE: RE: Did you know…?

Then what chance do we stand?

$$\boxtimes$$

FROM: Dan Jones
(mailto: dan@mcpl-media.co.uk)
TO: martin.davies@quantumfinance.co.uk
SENT: 14:06, Tuesday September 11, 2001
SUBJECT: Oh my god

Tell me you are near a television.

$$\boxtimes$$

FROM: Martin Davies
(mailto: martin.davies@quantumfinance.co.uk)
TO: dan@mcpl-media.co.uk
SENT: 14:06, Tuesday September 11, 2001
SUBJECT: RE: Oh my god

I'm not. Why?

⊠

FROM: Dan Jones
(mailto: dan@mcpl-media.co.uk)
TO: martin.davies@quantumfinance.co.uk
SENT: 14:06, Tuesday September 11, 2001
SUBJECT: RE: RE: Oh my god

There are planes crashing into America.

⊠

FROM: Martin Davies
(mailto: martin.davies@quantumfinance.co.uk)
TO: dan@mcpl-media.co.uk
SENT: 14:07, Tuesday September 11, 2001
SUBJECT: RE: RE: RE: Oh my god

You know I'm not near a television. Is this going to be
like when you told me the Pope had died, and I told
everyone in college that the Pope was dead, and they
all laughed at me?

⊠

FROM: Lloyd Thomas
(mailto: lloydt@callotech.co.uk)
TO: martin.davies@quantumfinance.co.uk
SENT: 14:07, Tuesday September 11, 2001
SUBJECT: F**king hell

Go to a news website. There's all kinds of $hit happening in New York.

⊠

FROM: Dan Jones
(mailto: dan@mcpl-media.co.uk)
TO: martin.davies@quantumfinance.co.uk
SENT: 14:07, Tuesday September 11, 2001
SUBJECT: RE: RE: RE: RE: Oh my god

I'm not joking, MD. Two f**king planes have gone into the twin towers. One crashed about twenty minutes ago, so there was a newsflash on BBC News 24... Well, you know what I mean. Not a newsflash exactly because it's a news channel. Just a flash, I suppose. And as they were showing the fire coming out of the tower, another plane came and went SMACK right into the other tower. Un-f**king-believable.

⊠

FROM: Lisa Cullis
(mailto: l.cullis@portersimpsonporter.co.uk)
TO: martin.davies@quantumfinance.co.uk
SENT: 14:08, Tuesday September 11, 2001
SUBJECT: Crumbs

Are you watching telly?

✉

FROM: Martin Davies
(mailto: martin.davies@quantumfinance.co.uk)
TO: l.cullis@portersimpsonporter.co.uk
SENT: 14:08, Tuesday September 11, 2001
SUBJECT: RE: Crumbs

No, but I've been told about it. What's happening?

✉

FROM: Martin Davies
(mailto: martin.davies@quantumfinance.co.uk)
TO: lloydt@callotech.co.uk
SENT: 14:08, Tuesday September 11, 2001
SUBJECT: RE: F**king Hell

Dan just told me about it. What's happening?

✉

FROM: Lisa Cullis
(mailto: l.cullis@portersimpsonporter.co.uk)
TO: martin.davies@quantumfinance.co.uk
SENT: 14:09, Tuesday September 11, 2001
SUBJECT: RE: RE: Crumbs

It's f**king madness. Buildings on fire, people running around all over the place. Brought me right down, it has. Jase is loving it. He thinks it's the funniest thing he's ever seen.

⊠

FROM: Martin Davies
(mailto: martin.davies@quantumfinance.co.uk)
TO: dan@mcpl-media.co.uk;
lloydt@callotech.co.uk
SENT: 14:10, Tuesday September 11, 2001
SUBJECT: What's going on?

What's going on?

⊠

FROM: Lloyd Thomas
(mailto: lloydt@callotech.co.uk)
TO: martin.davies@quantumfinance.co.uk
SENT: 14:11, Tuesday September 11, 2001
SUBJECT: RE: What's going on?

Nothing much. There's lots of smoke. Lots of fire. Lots of people screaming.
Who's Dan?

⊠

FROM: Dan Jones
(mailto: dan@mcpl-media.co.uk)
TO: martin.davies@quantumfinance.co.uk
SENT: 14:11, Tuesday September 11, 2001
SUBJECT: RE: What's going on?

It's absolute f**king chaos over there. Fire engines left right and centre. There's people still stuck in the towers, they reckon, but they can't land helicopters because of all the smoke. I have never seen anything like it in my life.

$\boxtimes$

FROM: Martin Davies
(mailto: martin.davies@quantumfinance.co.uk)
TO: lloydt@callotech.co.uk
SENT: 14:12, Tuesday September 11, 2001
SUBJECT: RE: RE: What's going on?

Dan's a mate from school. He lives in London.

$\boxtimes$

FROM: Lloyd Thomas
(mailto: lloydt@callotech.co.uk)
TO: martin.davies@quantumfinance.co.uk
SENT: 14:13, Tuesday September 11, 2001
SUBJECT: RE: RE: RE: What's going on?

You've never mentioned him before.

$\boxtimes$

FROM: Martin Davies
(mailto: martin.davies@quantumfinance.co.uk)
TO: lloydt@callotech.co.uk
SENT: 14:13, Tuesday September 11, 2001
SUBJECT: RE: RE: RE: RE: What's going on?

He's a school friend. He's lived in London for six years.
You haven't met him.

✉

FROM: Lloyd Thomas
(mailto: lloydt@callotech.co.uk)
TO: martin.davies@quantumfinance.co.uk
SENT: 14:14, Tuesday September 11, 2001
SUBJECT: RE: RE: RE: RE: RE: What's going on?

You don't have other friends. We're your friends.

✉

FROM: Corporate Communications
TO: All subjects
SENT: 14:16, Tuesday September 11, 2001
SUBJECT: Fourth floor access

Staff are reminded that the fourth floor is out-of-bounds
while it is not in use. We have recently been made
aware of incidents in which staff from lower floors have
been going to the fourth floor during lunch breaks and
outside of working hours. Be aware that this is in no

way permitted, and could result in disciplinary action. Furthermore, CCTV cameras have been installed on the stairwells, so security staff will be able to identify those staff who are not adhering to this rule.

Thank you.

⊠

FROM: Darren Andrews
TO: Martin Davies
SENT: 14:17, Tuesday September 11, 2001
SUBJECT: FW: Fourth floor access

They're talking about all the dogging that's been going on up there.

⊠

FROM: Martin Davies
TO: Darren Andrews
SENT: 14:17, Tuesday September 11, 2001
SUBJECT: RE: FW: Fourth floor access

Dogging?

⊠

FROM: Darren Andrews
TO: Martin Davies
SENT: 14:18, Tuesday September 11, 2001
SUBJECT: RE: RE: FW: Fourth floor access

Oh yeah. People have been fvcking up there, big time.
Mark Tamworth took Kelly Hatton up there last week. All
the people on the third floor go up there. Mark said that
as he was coming down the stairs, Steve Chicken and
Laura thingy off collections were on their way up.

✉

FROM: Martin Davies
TO: Darren Andrews
SENT: 14:18, Tuesday September 11, 2001
SUBJECT: RE: RE: RE: FW: Fourth floor access

Mark Tamworth has f**ked Kelly Hatton?

✉

FROM: Darren Andrews
TO: Martin Davies
SENT: 14:19, Tuesday September 11, 2001
SUBJECT: RE: RE: RE: RE: FW: Fourth floor
            access

Oh yeah. Big time. They're not seeing each other, like,
because her boyfriend's still banged up, and Mark said
they didn't actually sh*g, Kelly just blew him off.

✉

FROM: Martin Davies
TO: Darren Andrews
SENT: 14:20, Tuesday September 11, 2001
SUBJECT: RE: RE: RE: RE: RE: FW: Fourth floor
             access

But how? Mark's disgusting. How could she even touch him?

☒

FROM: Darren Andrews
TO: Martin Davies
SENT: 14:20, Tuesday September 11, 2001
SUBJECT: RE: RE: RE: RE: RE: RE: FW: Fourth
             floor access

Steady on, m8. Mark's one of the boys. Besides, don't tell me you wouldn't let Kelly Hatton blow you off.

☒

FROM: Martin Davies
TO: Darren Andrews
SENT: 14:21, Tuesday September 11, 2001
SUBJECT: RE: RE: RE: RE: RE: RE: RE: FW:
             Fourth floor access

That's immaterial. She's only, what, seventeen? Eighteen? And he must be thirty two by now.
    I feel sick.
    Have you heard about New York?

☒

FROM: Darren Andrews
TO: Martin Davies
SENT: 14:22, Tuesday September 11, 2001
SUBJECT: RE: RE: RE: RE: RE: RE: RE: RE: FW:
           Fourth floor access

Just spoke to one of my m8s. He said there's been a plane crash or something.

✉

FROM: Lisa Cullis
(mailto: l.cullis@portersimpsonporter.co.uk)
TO: martin.davies@quantumfinance.co.uk
SENT: 14:23, Tuesday September 11, 2001
SUBJECT: Jumpers

Martin... You're a media type person, or at least you want to be.

Sorry... does that sound a bit harsh?

Anyway... My question is this... Are they allowed to show people jumping off a burning building, even on the news? Jase and I were wondering this. Mark has left the office, because apparently his wife is on a shopping-and-Broadway weekend in New York with her sister, so he's absolutely CRAPPING himself. Am I allowed to say crapping?

F**k it.

Anyway... what I was saying was – are they allowed to show people jumping off a burning building, even for the news, because that's what they're showing, and if I wasn't coked up to the eyeballs it would probably be too much. I mean, these people are thousands of feet in the air. Even with the biggest trampoline in the world, nobody is going to survive that. It's all mildly perturbing.

✉

FROM: martin.davies@quantumfinance.co.uk
TO:
SAVED: 14:25, Tuesday September 11, 2001
SUBJECT:

Dear Aneurin

I am a twenty-six-year-old writer living in Cardiff. I have recently written a screenplay, provisionally titled 'The Meeting'. It is about a gay policeman in Cardiff investigating the grisly death of a teenage male prostitute, whose body has been found on waste ground near the old docks. His investigations lead him to a local celebrity astrologer and mystic, thereby uncovering a secret organisation of occultists living and working in the capital.

Then planes start crashing into America.

FUKCFUCKFUCKFUCKFUCKFUCKFUCKC-FUFCKFJFC

SAVED IN 'DRAFTS'

✉

FROM: martin.davies@quantumfinance.co.uk
TO:
SAVED: 14:26, Tuesday September 11, 2001
SUBJECT:

I wish I didn't feel so excited about all this.

SAVED IN 'DRAFTS'

✉

FROM: martin.davies@quantumfinance.co.uk
TO:
SAVED: 14:28, Tuesday September 11, 2001
SUBJECT:

Sometimes I watch you staring into space, like there's some kind of answer hanging there, and it looks as though you're about to start crying. It was a moment like that when I fell in love with you. I took a deep breath, and I realised that I never wanted to take my eyes off you, and that I was only happy when I was thinking about you.

   The beauty you put into my world is like that first bit of sunlight you get after a storm. Everything in my head is such a mess right now

SAVED IN 'DRAFTS'

✉

FROM: Lloyd Thomas
(mailto: lloydt@callotech.co.uk)
TO: martin.davies@quantumfinance.co.uk
SENT: 14:28, Tuesday September 11, 2001
SUBJECT: New York

It's typical. F**king news channels – They just show the same footage over and over again. Smoke coming out of the towers. Someone jumping off one of the towers. The second plane crashing into the tower. Three clips, that's all BBC, ITV, or f**king CNN have got. Fox News have one more bit of footage – A group of people on the ground screaming as the second plane crashes into the tower. They're all sitting at tables outside Starbucks sipping their mochas and looking up at the sky. What the f**k is the world coming to?

✉

FROM: Katherine Charles
TO: Andrews, Darren; Aziz, Safina; Davies,
             Martin; Gough, Lisa; Williamson,
             Joanne
SENT: 14:31, Tuesday September 11, 2001
SUBJECT: Shift swap

Hi everyone

Could anyone swap my 10-6 shift next Tuesday (Sept
18th) for a 9-5, only I'm supposed to be taking my niece
to the pictures and I've got to get home to pick her up.

Cheers

Katie

⊠

FROM: Lisa Cullis
(mailto: l.cullis@portersimpsonporter.co.uk)
TO: martin.davies@quantumfinance.co.uk
SENT: 14:34, Tuesday September 11, 2001
SUBJECT: What do you reckon?

I think it's terrorists.
    Jase thinks it's a really really bizarre coincidence, or
maybe that there's been some sort of massive
computer error, you know, like when they said the
Millennium Bug was going to hit us and all the planes
were going to start falling out of the sky.
    What do you reckon?

⊠

FROM: Lloyd Thomas
(mailto: lloydt@callotech.co.uk)
TO: martin.davies@quantumfinance.co.uk
SENT: 14:35, Tuesday September 11, 2001
SUBJECT: Phobias

Hypsophobia – A fear of high places
Acrophobia – A fear of heights
?

✉

FROM: Safina Aziz
TO: Martin Davies
SENT: 14:38, Tuesday September 11, 2001
SUBJECT: Wedding

Have you given it any more thought? I'd love you to be there. It'll be nice not to have to speak Urdu all day, because my Urdu is rubbish. I don't know what I'm going to be like on honeymoon. I'll be asking for everything in English!!

✉

FROM: Lloyd Thomas
(mailto: lloydt@callotech.co.uk)
TO: martin.davies@quantumfinance.co.uk
SENT: 14:40, Tuesday September 11, 2001
SUBJECT: Even more phobias

Apeirophobia – A fear of infinity
Chronophobia – A fear of duration
Cherophobia – A fear of cheerfulness
Ataxiophobia – A fear of disorder

✉

FROM: Dan Jones
(mailto: dan@mcpl-media.co.uk)
TO: Martin Davies
SENT: 14:43, Tuesday September 11, 2001
SUBJECT:

This is just unbelievable. They're saying another plane has crashed, this time into the Pentagon. The f**king Pentagon! I can't believe it. I just can't believe it.

✉

FROM: Lisa Cullis
(mailto: l.cullis@portersimpsonporter.co.uk)
TO: martin.davies@quantumfinance.co.uk
SENT: 14:45, Tuesday September 11, 2001
SUBJECT: Whoops!

Another plane has crashed, only this one's crashed into the Octagon, or whatever that building's called.

Well… That's ended Jase's latest theory – that it was all a CIA conspiracy. Why crash a plane into your own office? I've told him this. He reckons everyone in the Pentagon is probably on holiday or was on lunch. I pointed out to him that over there it is only something like half past nine. He now reckons they're out on breakfast.

I told him there's no such phrase as 'on breakfast', or even 'to breakfast', but he's having none of it. Tell him he's wrong, Martin. Email him on j.webb@portersimpsonporter.co.uk and tell him what a stupid wrong man he is.

✉

FROM: Susan Meredith
TO: Martin Davies
SENT: 14:48, Tuesday September 11, 2001
SUBJECT: Meeting

Martin

Tony just called to let me know that he might be running a little late, so the meeting might not be until about ten past, maybe quarter past five. Hope that's okay with you.

Sue

⊠

FROM: martin.davies@quantumfinance.co.uk
TO:
SAVED: 14:49, Tuesday September 11, 2001
SUBJECT: Meeting

Sue,

I'm closing my eyes and asking myself the question, DO I GIVE A FUCK?
    There are planes crashing into America, Sue. It sounds small now, but I know it's going to be big. Tony can be ten minutes, fifteen minutes, ninety minutes late. I don't care.
    What would we do if a plane crashed into us?

SAVED IN 'DRAFTS'

⊠

FROM: Lloyd Thomas
(mailto: lloydt@callotech.co.uk)
TO: martin.davies@quantumfinance.co.uk
SENT: 14:51, Tuesday September 11, 2001
SUBJECT: Place your bets

Okay… We've got a sweepstake going in work. Who do you reckon is behind this truly awful attack?

Weird right wing American types?

North Korea?

Iran?

China?

Cuba?

Russia?

Kiribati?

(I've only put Kiribati in to confuse Gareth who works on the presses. I've told him Kiribati is a rogue nation with biological and maybe nuclear weapons. Poor f**kwit hasn't got a clue.)

My money is riding on 'weird right wing American types', you know, in revenge for Waco or something. I've got a fiver on it.

✉

FROM: Lisa Cullis
(mailto: l.cullis@portersimpsonporter.co.uk)
TO: martin.davies@quantumfinance.co.uk
SENT: 14:54, Tuesday September 11, 2001
SUBJECT:

This is SO weird. From our window you can see Queen Street. There are loads of people stood outside Dixons, just staring at all the tellies in the windows, like something out of 'Dawn of the Dead'. Jase and I have stopped watching TV, and have started watching the people watching TV. They're all shaking their heads and talking into their mobiles.

Talking of 'Dawn of the Dead', have you got my copy of that in your room?

⊠

FROM: Dan Jones
(mailto: dan@mcpl-media.co.uk)
TO: martin.davies@quantumfinance.co.uk
SENT: 14:56, Tuesday September 11, 2001
SUBJECT:

They're stopping flights everywhere. One of our producers is stuck in Barcelona and they're cancelling every single flight. They've just evacuated the City of London and they're on about evacuating this place too. What's happening in Cardiff?

⊠

FROM: Martin Davies
(mailto: martin.davies@quantumfinance.co.uk)
TO: dan@mcpl-media.co.uk
SENT: 14:57, Tuesday September 11, 2001
SUBJECT: RE:

Nothing. Nothing's happening. None of the managers have even mentioned it. It's like it isn't happening at all. In fact, I'm not entirely sure it is.

⊠

FROM: Dan Jones
(mailto: dan@mcpl-media.co.uk)
TO: martin.davies@quantumfinance.co.uk
SENT: 14:59, Tuesday September 11, 2001
SUBJECT: RE: RE:

I'm watching people jumping out of burning buildings.
This is happening, Martin.

$$\boxtimes$$

FROM: Martin Davies
(mailto: martin.davies@quantumfinance.co.uk)
TO: dan@mcpl-media.co.uk
SENT: 15:00, Tuesday September 11, 2001
SUBJECT: RE: RE: RE:

Not here, it isn't. Not in this building. Nothing happens
in this building. Not time. Not death.
Nothing.

$$\boxtimes$$

FROM: Lloyd Thomas
(mailto: lloydt@callotech.co.uk)
TO: martin.davies@quantumfinance.co.uk
SENT: 15:02, Tuesday September 11, 2001
SUBJECT: Even MORE phobias

Algophobia – A fear of pain
Satanophobia – A fear of Satan
Automysophobia – A fear of being dirty
Chrometophobia – A fear of money
Coitophobia – A fear of having 5ex
Eosophobia – A fear of dawn

$$\boxtimes$$

FROM: Lisa Cullis
(mailto: l.cullis@portersimpsonporter.co.uk)
TO: martin.davies@quantumfinance.co.uk
SENT: 15:04, Tuesday September 11, 2001
SUBJECT:

Jase has opened the window and he's shouting, "Fire!" at the top of his voice.

He was lying to me in Ha Ha's when he said he'd run out of coke. He had a half-gram wrap in his wallet, so we're tucking into that before it's home time. He's been cutting out lines on his desk with a Marks & Spencers storecard. I hope Mark doesn't come back.

Is Lloyd coming out on Saturday? I'm just wondering if it'll make things weird. I've spoken to Sara and she thinks it will.

✉

FROM: Martin Davies
(mailto: martin.davies@quantumfinance.co.uk)
TO: l.cullis@portersimpsonporter.co.uk
SENT: 15:05, Tuesday September 11, 2001
SUBJECT: RE:

Okay... cut the hush-hush rubbish... What happened between you and Lloyd at the barbecue? And what's it got to do with Sara? Did you f**k him? Did she f**k him?

✉

FROM: Lisa Cullis
(mailto: l.cullis@portersimpsonporter.co.uk)
TO: martin.davies@quantumfinance.co.uk
SENT: 15:05, Tuesday September 11, 2001
SUBJECT: RE: RE:

Did he tell you that?

✉

FROM: Martin Davies
(mailto: martin.davies@quantumfinance.co.uk)
TO: l.cullis@portersimpsonporter.co.uk
SENT: 15:06, Tuesday September 11, 2001
SUBJECT: RE: RE: RE:

No.
You just did.

✉

FROM: Dan Jones
(mailto: dan@mcpl-media.co.uk)
TO: martin.davies@quantumfinance.co.uk
SENT: 15:06, Tuesday September 11, 2001
SUBJECT: RE: RE: RE: RE:

Then move to London.
     Not today, obviously. They seem to be evacuating everywhere and the traffic is becoming a nightmare.
     But move here. I miss seeing you around.

✉

FROM: Lisa Cullis
(mailto: l.cullis@portersimpsonporter.co.uk)
TO: martin.davies@quantumfinance.co.uk
SENT: 15:07, Tuesday September 11, 2001
SUBJECT: RE: RE: RE: RE:

Well I didn't f**k him, and neither did Sara. But things happened. We were upstairs, in my bedroom. Sara was skinning up and Lloyd was chopping up lines of coke on my mirror. We all started getting a bit cuddly, and then next thing you know items of clothing were being taken off. It didn't mean anything. Lloyd's really funny, and kind of sweet, but now it's a bit weird. We all kind of agreed that we wouldn't really talk about it, so don't you say a word to him.

⊠

FROM: Martin Davies
(mailto: martin.davies@quantumfinance.co.uk)
TO: l.cullis@portersimpsonporter.co.uk
SENT: 15:07, Tuesday September 11, 2001
SUBJECT: RE: RE: RE: RE: RE:

You had a threesome?

⊠

FROM: Lisa Cullis
(mailto: l.cullis@portersimpsonporter.co.uk)
TO: martin.davies@quantumfinance.co.uk
SENT: 15:08, Tuesday September 11, 2001
SUBJECT: RE: RE: RE: RE: RE: RE:

It wasn't a threesome exactly, Martin. Lloyd licked Sara out and I sucked him off. There wasn't any lezzer stuff and we didn't spit-roast him. Now Jase and I are going to finish off this coke and shout at the tourists for a bit.
  Ciao

FROM: Lloyd Thomas
(mailto: lloydt@callotech.co.uk)
TO: martin.davies@quantumfinance.co.uk
SENT: 15:09, Tuesday September 11, 2001
SUBJECT: Bl**dy Palestinians

According to Abu Dhabi Television there has been an anonymous call claiming responsibility for the terrorist attacks on behalf of the Democratic Front For The Liberation Of Palestine. Not very Democratic, in my book. Bl**dy typical, isn't it? We had right wing nutters, North Koreans, Iranians, the Chinese, the Russians..... Didn't think of the f**king Palestinians, did we? Always with a new trick up their sleeves.......
  Well, all bets are off.

FROM: Safina Aziz
TO: Martin Davies
SENT: 15:11, Tuesday September 11, 2001
SUBJECT: Wedding

I'll take you not saying anything as a 'no thanks' then.

✉

FROM: martin.davies@quantumfinance.co.uk
TO:
SAVED: 15:12, Tuesday September 11, 2001
SUBJECT: RE: Wedding

It's not a 'no thanks' like you think it is. I don't know what's happening to me today.
    I do know what's happening to me today.
    I don't know what's going to happen to me today.
    I'm sorry

SAVED IN 'DRAFTS'

✉

FROM: martin.davies@quantumfinance.co.uk
TO: theresa.ogorman@hotmail.com
SENT: 15:14, Tuesday September 11, 2001
SUBJECT: you

Theresa

Long time no see. How's things with you? Life here in Cardiff is same-old same-old, you know how it is! Lloyd is getting up to his usual tricks. The new house is ok. We've got noisy next door neighbours, but then who hasn't?! The garden's nice. Not that ours wasn't, but it's nice in the same way. I miss seeing you around. I don't mean that in a creepy way. I miss seeing you.

I miss you.

I don't know what happened. I thought we were okay. Was there anything I could have done? I thought when people broke up it was for reasons. You know... someone's had an affair or somebody isn't pulling their weight. Was there something I could have done? I miss you.

All my passwords in work are still you, they're still your name. We change them once a month, so I could have changed them, but they're still you. I've still got your photo as the wallpaper on my pc at home.

You're not like a person I don't see any more. You're like a colour that's suddenly gone. As if somebody took away the colour blue or the colour red. I walk through each day doing the same things I ever did, but there's something missing, and if I think about it I realise it's you.

I miss you so much.

Martin xx

✉

FROM: Martin Davies
(mailto: martin.davies@quantumfinance.co.uk)
TO: lloydt@callotech.co.uk
SENT: 15:15, Tuesday September 11, 2001
SUBJECT: Categories

I'm category two. Does that answer your f**king question?

⊠

FROM: Dan Jones
(mailto: dan@mcpl-media.co.uk)
TO: martin.davies@quantumfinance.co.uk
SENT: 15:16, Tuesday September 11, 2001
SUBJECT: Sorry

Sorry if I came on a bit strong in the last email. I know
it's all water under the bridge and everything. Not even
water under the bridge. It's ancient history.
  One of the twin towers has collapsed, by the way.
They don't know how many people were inside it, but
they think it could be thousands. They're saying that
another plane has crashed, too, but it hasn't hit anything
except the ground. The planes are just dropping out of
the sky.

⊠

FROM: Martin Davies
(mailto: martin.davies@quantumfinance.co.uk)
TO: dan@mcpl-media.co.uk
SENT: 15:16, Tuesday September 11, 2001
SUBJECT: RE: Sorry

What's ancient history?

⊠

FROM: Dan Jones
(mailto: dan@mcpl-media.co.uk)
TO: martin.davies@quantumfinance.co.uk
SENT: 15:19, Tuesday September 11, 2001
SUBJECT: RE: RE: Sorry

Bristol.

✉

FROM: Martin Davies
(mailto: martin.davies@quantumfinance.co.uk)
TO: dan@mcpl-media.co.uk
SENT: 15:21, Tuesday September 11, 2001
SUBJECT: RE: RE: RE: Sorry

Bristol? That was years ago.

✉

FROM: Lloyd Thomas
(mailto: lloydt@callotech.co.uk)
TO: martin.davies@quantumfinance.co.uk
SENT: 15:22, Tuesday September 11, 2001
SUBJECT: RE: Categories

Yes it does. Oh, and apparently it wasn't the Palestinians. They think it's that guy with the turban and the beard, Osmond something-or-other.
Atephobia – A fear of ruin
Peccatophobia – A fear of sin
Hedonophobia – A fear of pleasure
Teratophobia – A fear of monsters
Nyctophobia – A fear of darkness
Pantophobia – A fear of everything

✉

FROM: Dan Jones
(mailto: dan@mcpl-media.co.uk)
TO: martin.davies@quantumfinance.co.uk
SENT: 15:25, Tuesday September 11, 2001
SUBJECT: RE: RE: RE: RE: Sorry

I'm sorry. I know… Off limits, and all the rest of it. Maybe all that partying you've been getting up to means you don't remember things as well as I do. I know we're older but they're still my memories.

✉

FROM: Lloyd Thomas
(mailto: lloydt@callotech.co.uk)
TO: martin.davies@quantumfinance.co.uk
SENT: 15:28, Tuesday September 11, 2001
SUBJECT: Men in horn-rimmed glasses

I was just thinking, when people look back on the footage of today, who will the Men In Horned Rim Glasses be?

Let me explain:

When you look at all the footage of the events surrounding the assassination of JFK, check out just how many Men In Horn Rimmed Glasses (or MIHRGs) you can see. There are thousands of the ba$tards. Abraham Zapruder, the guy who shot the famous footage – Horn-Rimmed Glasses. Earl Warren, the guy behind the Warren Commission – Horn-Rimmed Glasses. What does Walter Kronkite do when he tells the nation that JFK is dead… He takes off his Horn-Rimmed Glasses.

I think today is going to be historic. One of the f**king twin towers has COLLAPSED, dude. They'll be showing this on TV for YEARS. So what's the 'look' going to be?

I think it's going to be fat women in franchise restaurant t-shirts. They keep showing footage of people running away from this f**k-off-sized cloud of smoke and dust, and I swear… they're all fat women in franchise restaurant t-shirts.

Hard Rock Café.

Planet Hollywood.

Kenny Rogers Chickens.

All of them running and screaming like characters in a Godzilla film.

⊠

FROM: Dan Jones
(mailto: dan@mcpl-media.co.uk)
TO: martin.davies@quantumfinance.co.uk
SENT: 15:30, Tuesday September 11, 2001
SUBJECT: RE: RE: RE: RE: Sorry

The second tower has collapsed.

⊠

FROM: Martin Davies
(mailto: martin.davies@quantumfinance.co.uk)
TO: l.cullis@portersimpsonporter.co.uk
SENT: 15:32, Tuesday September 11, 2001
SUBJECT: Last night

Can you remember that crazy tramp guy who came up to us on Mill Lane last night? He said the world was going to end today, didn't he?

⊠

FROM: Lloyd Thomas
(mailto: lloydt@callotech.co.uk)
TO: martin.davies@quantumfinance.co.uk
SENT: 15:34, Tuesday September 11, 2001
SUBJECT:

Auroraphobia – A fear of the Northern Lights. (I'm guessing that doesn't affect that many people outside of the Arctic Circle. Actually, I'm guessing it doesn't affect that many people full stop. But imagine the bad luck of being one of the people who gets affected, and being born in Norway, or Alaska or something. That would suck.)

You've gone radio silent. Have I done a baddy?

✉

FROM: Dan Jones
(mailto: dan@mcpl-media.co.uk)
TO: martin.davies@quantumfinance.co.uk
SENT: 15:35, Tuesday September 11, 2001
SUBJECT:

They're already saying there may have been 10,000 people in and around the World Trade Centre. This is just unbelievable. I can't believe it's real.

✉

FROM: martin.davies@quantumfinance.co.uk
TO:
SAVED: 15:35, Tuesday September 11, 2001
SUBJECT:

It's not real

SAVED IN 'DRAFTS'

FROM: Martin Davies
(mailto: martin.davies@quantumfinance.co.uk)
TO: lloydt@callotech.co.uk
SENT: 15:36, Tuesday September 11, 2001
SUBJECT: RE:

Lisa told me about the barbecue.

FROM: Lloyd Thomas
(mailto: lloydt@callotech.co.uk)
TO: martin.davies@quantumfinance.co.uk
SENT: 15:36, Tuesday September 11, 2001
SUBJECT: RE: RE:

Oh.

FROM: Lisa Cullis
(mailto: l.cullis@portersimpsonporter.co.uk)
TO: martin.davies@quantumfinance.co.uk
SENT: 15:37, Tuesday September 11, 2001
SUBJECT: RE: Last night

What crazy tramp? When were we on Mill Lane? Last
night, is this?

⊠

FROM: Martin Davies
(mailto: martin.davies@quantumfinance.co.uk)
TO: lloydt@callotech.co.uk
SENT: 15:37, Tuesday September 11, 2001
SUBJECT: RE: RE: RE:

Is it possible for you to meet a woman without f**king
them?

⊠

FROM: Lloyd Thomas
(mailto: lloydt@callotech.co.uk)
TO: martin.davies@quantumfinance.co.uk
SENT: 15:38, Tuesday September 11, 2001
SUBJECT: RE: RE: RE: RE:

I didn't f**k them. Lisa gave me a blowy and I went
down on Sara.

⊠

FROM: Martin Davies
(mailto: martin.davies@quantumfinance.co.uk)
TO: lloydt@callotech.co.uk
SENT: 15:38, Tuesday September 11, 2001
SUBJECT: RE: RE: RE: RE: RE:

Oh my God. Why does everyone seem to think the tech-
nicalities of this are so f**king important? You did naked
things with my housemates. That's the issue here.

⊠

FROM: Lloyd Thomas
(mailto: lloydt@callotech.co.uk)
TO: martin.davies@quantumfinance.co.uk
SENT: 15:39, Tuesday September 11, 2001
SUBJECT: RE: RE: RE: RE: RE: RE:

You sound pi55ed off. You're not sh*gging either of
them, are you?

⊠

FROM: Dan Jones
(mailto: dan@mcpl-media.co.uk)
TO: martin.davies@quantumfinance.co.uk
SENT: 15:39, Tuesday September 11, 2001
SUBJECT:

They're saying now it could be as many as 20,000
people. The footage looks like something out of a film,
like 'Independence Day' or something. None of it feels
real. Can I call you later?

⊠

FROM: Martin Davies
(mailto: martin.davies@quantumfinance.co.uk)
TO: lloydt@callotech.co.uk
SENT: 15:42, Tuesday September 11, 2001
SUBJECT: RE: RE: RE: RE: RE: RE: RE:

I'm not "sh*gging" either of them, it's just that you consume everything. It's like you've got this "ultimate shopper" mentality. It doesn't exist unless you've owned it, tasted it, f**ked it.

They're my friends, and you're my friend, and now you might have gone and f**ked the whole lot of it, just so you could all rub genitals in each other's faces.
What was it meant to be? Some cool, detached, drug-f**ked thing – so post-ironic that none of you even came?

"We're all so epitome-of-cool we don't even FEEL anything about this…"

But none of that works out on Tuesday, does it? When the drugs have worn off and your real, grubby little emotions like jealousy and resentment kick back in.

✉

FROM: Martin Davies
(mailto: martin.davies@quantumfinance.co.uk)
TO: l.cullis@portersimpsonporter.co.uk
SENT: 15:44, Tuesday September 11, 2001
SUBJECT: RE: RE: Last night

There was a tramp. He came up to us. He told us to max all our credit cards and empty all of our bank accounts, because today was going to be the end of the world. Can't you remember him?

✉

FROM: Dan Jones
(mailto: dan@mcpl-media.co.uk)
TO: martin.davies@quantumfinance.co.uk
SENT: 15:44, Tuesday September 11, 2001
SUBJECT:

I'm sorry I brought it up. It's just that we've never talked about what happened, and maybe there wasn't anything to really talk about, but I think it's put a bit of a wedge between us. Even when you've come down to visit there's been this detachment, and I always thought I'd done something wrong. Stacey's noticed it, when you've been around. It's like we're forcing ourselves to have fun, because we've been mates for years, but that something isn't right, and I don't know whether I'm right, but I've always thought it was Bristol. Can I call you tonight?

✉

FROM: Jenni Baker
TO: Martin Davies
SENT: 15:45, Tuesday September 11, 2001
SUBJECT: LP6 Reports

Hi Martyn,

You'll find attached the LP6 reports for September. It's been a slow month, but we're expecting business to pick back up in October, as Kelly's Design have a promotion starting on Oct 10th.
    Hope these are helpful.

    Regards

    Jenni
lp6_reports/file

✉

FROM: Martin Davies
TO: Jenni Baker
SENT: 15:45, Tuesday September 11, 2001
SUBJECT: RE: LP6 Reports

I think this was meant for Martyn Davies in Information Retrieval. I'm Martin Davies.

⊠

FROM: Martin Davies
(mailto: martin.davies@quantumfinance.co.uk)
TO: dan@mcpl-media.co.uk
SENT: 15:46, Tuesday September 11, 2001
SUBJECT: RE:

I'm sorry. I didn't think there was much to discuss. Things happen when you're younger. I didn't realise you still thought about it.

⊠

FROM: Dan Jones
(mailto: dan@mcpl-media.co.uk)
TO: martin.davies@quantumfinance.co.uk
SENT: 15:46, Tuesday September 11, 2001
SUBJECT: RE: RE:

Which I take it means you don't.

⊠

FROM: Lloyd Thomas
(mailto: lloydt@callotech.co.uk)
TO: martin.davies@quantumfinance.co.uk
SENT: 15:48, Tuesday September 11, 2001
SUBJECT: RE: RE: RE: RE: RE: RE: RE: RE:

You're actually pi$$ed off with me? You're not joking?

✉

FROM: Martin Davies
(mailto: martin.davies@quantumfinance.co.uk)
TO: dan@mcpl-media.co.uk
SENT: 15:48, Tuesday September 11, 2001
SUBJECT: RE: RE: RE:

It's not that I don't think about it. It's just not a part of who I am, and I didn't think it was a part of who you were. You live with Stacey.

✉

FROM: Martin Davies
(mailto: martin.davies@quantumfinance.co.uk)
TO: lloydt@callotech.co.uk
SENT: 15:49, Tuesday September 11, 2001
SUBJECT: RE: RE: RE: RE: RE: RE: RE: RE: RE:

YES, I'm pi$$ed off with you. Is it that hard to grasp that somebody is actually pi$$ed off with you, and that your cheeky grin and your 'aw shucks I'm sorry' face isn't going to f**king work this time?
Did you ever try it on with Theresa?

✉

FROM: Lisa Cullis
(mailto: l.cullis@portersimpsonporter.co.uk)
TO: martin.davies@quantumfinance.co.uk
SENT: 15:49, Tuesday September 11, 2001
SUBJECT: Tramp

So there was a crazy tramp who came up to us on Mill Lane and told us the world was going to end? Are you sure?

　　Freaky.

⊠

FROM: Lloyd Thomas
(mailto: lloydt@callotech.co.uk)
TO: martin.davies@quantumfinance.co.uk
SENT: 15:50, Tuesday September 11, 2001
SUBJECT: RE: RE: RE: RE: RE: RE: RE: RE: RE: RE:

What?

⊠

FROM: Martin Davies
(mailto: martin.davies@quantumfinance.co.uk)
TO: lloydt@callotech.co.uk
SENT: 15:50, Tuesday September 11, 2001
SUBJECT: RE: RE: RE: RE: RE: RE: RE: RE: RE: RE: RE:

DID YOU TRY IT ON WITH THERESA?
Did you try and f**k her?

⊠

FROM: Dan Jones
(mailto: dan@mcpl-media.co.uk)
TO: martin.davies@quantumfinance.co.uk
SENT: 15:51, Tuesday September 11, 2001
SUBJECT: RE: RE: RE: RE:

Then I guess I'm being really stupid. I just had a moment, not that long ago, when I thought about the time you visited me in Bristol, and I realised I've never been happier than that weekend. We were walking down the Christmas Steps, both of us drunk, and I realised I wasn't worried about anything. There wasn't a thing in my mind that could hurt me or lose me any sleep. And you were walking with me. We got back to mine, and for a while we just lay there, drunk and giggling. I thought my heart was going to explode in my chest. Then you held my hand in yours. I was so f**king happy.

✉

FROM: Lloyd Thomas
(mailto: lloydt@callotech.co.uk)
TO: martin.davies@quantumfinance.co.uk
SENT: 15:52, Tuesday September 11, 2001
SUBJECT: RE: RE: RE: RE: RE: RE: RE: RE: RE: RE: RE: RE:

What a thing to ask. You're my m8. I'd never do a thing like that.

✉

FROM: Martin Davies
(mailto: martin.davies@quantumfinance.co.uk)
TO: lloydt@callotech.co.uk
SENT: 15:52, Tuesday September 11, 2001
SUBJECT: RE: RE: RE: RE: RE: RE: RE: RE: RE:
             RE: RE: RE:RE:

She said "no", didn't she?

⊠

FROM: Gini Mayhew
TO: Business Maintenance Users
SENT: 15:52, Tuesday September 11, 2001
SUBJECT: Congratulations

Congratulations to Lisa Gough on getting her Stage 3
Mandate. This is a reflection of the hard work of Lisa
and her mentor, Simon. Well done, both!

⊠

FROM: Darren Andrews
TO: Martin Davies
SENT: 15:52, Tuesday September 11, 2001
SUBJECT: FW: Congratulations

That, and the fact that she's Tony Cuccinello's niece.

⊠

FROM: Toby Green
(tobester69@hotmail.com)
TO: mhurley@jamstar.com; dan@mcpl-
media.co.uk; friggyjo@yahoo.com;
randystyle@bringme.co.uk; quangvp@hotmail.com;
jizlober@fuckyou.co.uk; rowleyoda@inorbit.com;
bootifulstu@buzzmail.com; benjster@hemail.com;
martin.davies@quantumfinance.co.uk
SENT: 15:53, Tuesday September 11, 2001
SUBJECT: Postcard From Oz No. 6

Hi Guys

Sorry it's been a while, but you know how it is. Left Sydney on Thursday, travelling across the South Coast. We're currently in a town called Streaky Bay, which is just up the road from Anxious Bay. That's where the wallabies drink too much coffee ha ha.

Met some crazy guys from Canada who are lots of fun and drink lots of beer, so we're having lots of fun. Tomorrow we'll keep heading across the South Coast, driving through Nullabor National Park, and then on to Perth, though that'll take us another couple of days. After Perth we're thinking of flying up to Uluru National Park. Uluru is the Aboriginal name for Ayers Rock, apparently. Hope you are all well. How's your leg, Mat? Industrial accidents? I don't know! And how's Dan? Living the high life and sipping champagne with the upper echelons, I'll wager.

Congratulations about the baby, Jo!!!! Send me a photo! Glad to hear you're snowboarding again, Andy. I thought it was time you got back on the old board. Quang – What the hell are you up to these days? I haven't heard from you in AGES. Same goes for you, Goldsmith though someone told me you're doing STAND UP? Jiz – How the hell did YOU get a promotion, you crazy sod? Gav… You with a baby too! So many babies! Are we getting old or something? Ben –

An older woman, ay? You sly old dog. Martin – Sorry to hear about you and Theresa.

Well, gotta go now. They don't like people hogging their internet, out here in the sticks.

Tobes xxxx

FROM: Lloyd Thomas
(mailto: lloydt@callotech.co.uk)
TO: martin.davies@quantumfinance.co.uk
SENT: 15:55, Tuesday September 11, 2001
SUBJECT: Sorry

It was a party, and I got a bit drunk, and maybe I made a bit of a pass at her, but it was all innocent fun. I WOULDN'T HAVE DONE ANYTHING. I PROMISE.

FROM: Martin Davies
(mailto: martin.davies@quantumfinance.co.uk)
TO: lloydt@callotech.co.uk
SENT: 15:58, Tuesday September 11, 2001
SUBJECT: RE: Sorry

You can't promise something in retrospect. Life doesn't work that way. I knew you had tried something. She told me. Except she didn't tell me it was you.

She just said that something had happened... Something and nothing.

"Nothing happened," she said. "But it made me think about things."

Tell me you were jealous, please. Tell me you were green with envy and you hated the fact that I was happy, and you set out to destroy what I had. Tell me that, and at least I can see a reason. Tell me you did it all on purpose, to give me something to feel. Just please don't tell me what I know you're going to tell me: That it meant absolutely nothing to you.

✉

FROM: martin.davies@quantumfinance.co.uk
TO:
SAVED: 15:59, Tuesday September 11, 2001
SUBJECT:

Plans are nothing more than weak strings suspended between ideas you once had, and yet we treat them as walls and floors of re-enforced concrete. When they collapse and disintegrate, we stand back amazed, wondering how it could possibly have happened.

I thought my plans were strong enough to get me through, but they're not. They are gossamer. They are the first powdery snowflakes of January. Cobwebs break on a strong breeze and snowflakes thaw.
I have nothing.

SAVED IN 'DRAFTS'

✉

FROM: Dan Jones
(mailto: dan@mcpl-media.co.uk)
TO: martin.davies@quantumfinance.co.uk
SENT: 16:01, Tuesday September 11, 2001
SUBJECT:

It's hard to get your head around the idea that 20,000 people might be dead, don't you think?

It makes you think about things, and I suppose that's why I came out and said all that stuff earlier. You start thinking that if you don't say those things here and now, something will happen and you'll never get a chance to say it.

I love you. I've spent far too long not meaning it when I say that, and not caring when somebody says it to me. It's not that I even think you'd ever care as much about me. I just wanted you to know.

Somebody loves you, Martin Davies.

Xx

✉

FROM: Corporate Communications
TO: All subjects
SENT: 16:03, Tuesday September 11, 2001
SUBJECT: Splash A Boss Day

DON'T FORGET – THIS FRIDAY IS SPLASH-A-BOSS DAY! GET YOUR OWN BACK ON YOUR MANAGER WITH A WET SPONGE AND A BUCKET OF WATER! EVERY PENNY RAISED WILL BE GOING TO ST WINIFRED'S HOSPICE FOR THE TERMINALLY ILL, A CHARITY WHICH TAKES CARE OF THOSE WITH

CANCER AND HIV, ALONG WITH MANY OTHER TERMINAL ILLNESSES. CONTACT PORSCHA LEWIS FOR DETAILS.

✉

FROM: Lloyd Thomas
(mailto: lloydt@callotech.co.uk)
TO: martin.davies@quantumfinance.co.uk
SENT: 16:05, Tuesday September 11, 2001
SUBJECT: SORRY

Look… Martin… You know I wouldn't do anything to upset you. Not on purpose. We're the posse. Remember? West Side? Yo momma?

Remember?

Crazy Mo Fo's?

Why would I risk f**king that up? If I did anything it was drink, or pills, or coke, or whatever I'd had that night, and I think I'd had everything.

Come on, Martin… This is all ancient history we're talking about. Water under the bridge and all the rest of it.

If we aren't friends then I have no-one to tell all about keraunothnetophobia, which is the fear of falling man-made satellites… Or dysmorphophobia, the fear of disfigurement. Or gynophobia, the fear of women. And are we not ALL gynophobic at heart? At least a little bit?

They are another species, dude, and they do strange things to our minds, especially when we are drunk and we haven't even had a decent w@nk for a week. I live with two gay men, Martin. It's not easy catching a decent moment when you can watch p*rn without worrying about them listening. THE WALLS ARE PAPER THIN, FOR CRYING OUT LOUD.

I am sorry, Martin. I am SO sorry. I would crawl through broken glass and drink dog's pi$$ for you, you know this. What do I have to do to prove this to you?

✉

FROM: Martin Davies
(mailto: martin.davies@quantumfinance.co.uk)
TO: lloydt@callotech.co.uk
SENT: 16:07, Tuesday September 11, 2001
SUBJECT: RE: SORRY

Try crawling on broken glass and drinking dog's pi$$.

✉

FROM: Lisa Cullis
(mailto: l.cullis@portersimpsonporter.co.uk)
TO: martin.davies@quantumfinance.co.uk
SENT: 16:10, Tuesday September 11, 2001
SUBJECT:

Jase and I are going back to ours. Mark isn't coming back to the office. Maybe his wife has been hit by a plane. We're thinking we'll probably get tomorrow off work if she has. Sara knows someone who can get coke and maybe ketamine this evening, so we thought we'd make a night of it. Get a bottle of wine on your way home and I'll have a line waiting for you when you get in!

✉

FROM: Corporate Communications
TO: All subjects
SENT: 16:14, Tuesday September 11, 2001
SUBJECT: Operation DoGood

As you may or may not be aware, this year Quantum Finance will once more be taking part in Operation DoGood; a charity dedicated to helping the self-improvement of developing communities in the UK. Previous Operation DoGood projects have seen leisure centres refurbished, Youth Clubs established, and even a weekly cinema club started, at a community centre in Bridgend. This year the ball is in your court. What would you like to see Operation DoGood do in your community? Perhaps the eradication of graffiti, or a spot of landscape gardening in a nearby public park.

Five projects in the South Wales area will then be chosen from these suggestions, with those taking part in each project invited to a prize-giving ceremony in June 2002, to be attended by television weather girl Sian Lloyd.

So come on! What have you got to loose? You can post your suggestions on the intranet by going to CARDIFF / EVENTS / OPERATION DOGOOD.

Thank you.

⊠

FROM: martin.davies@quantumfinance.co.uk
TO:
SAVED: 16:16, Tuesday September 11, 2001
SUBJECT:

What if I don't want to be loved?

SAVED IN 'DRAFTS'

⊠

FROM: martin.davies@quantumfinance.co.uk
TO:
SAVED: 16:17, Tuesday September 11, 2001
SUBJECT:

What if I said I hated you all?

SAVED IN 'DRAFTS'

FROM: martin.davies@quantumfinance.co.uk
TO:
SAVED: 16:17, Tuesday September 11, 2001
SUBJECT:

I'm lying. It's not hate. Hate is an overused word. But am I not supposed to smile when I see your name on my phone? Am I not meant to look forward to seeing you again, maybe even counting down the hours until it happens?

   And I know I'm not meant to dread even the sound of your voice, but I do.

SAVED IN 'DRAFTS'

FROM: Dan Jones
(mailto: dan@mcpl-media.co.uk)
TO: martin.davies@quantumfinance.co.uk
SENT: 16:19, Tuesday September 11, 2001
SUBJECT: Oops

Okay, I said too much and I overstepped the mark. I know that.

I just want you to know that it's not like I want anything to happen, or anything, because I understand how things are. I just miss seeing you around, and it's you I miss, not the _____ – there's a word I'm looking for here, but I can't f**king think of it. Everything's a bit f**ked up right now. I've got my boss telling me they're thinking of evacuating the whole of Canary Wharf, which means we'll probably end up sipping tepid americanos in All Bar One waiting for the emergency to end.

What's the word I'm trying to think of… Dammit, can't think of a thing.

But it's not that that I miss… It's just you making me laugh. I mean, before the whole Theresa thing. Anyway, this is me extending the olive branch, and trying to repair all the weirdness, and hoping you're not too freaked out or anything.

x

✉

FROM: Safina Aziz
TO: Martin Davies
SENT: 16:20, Tuesday September 11, 2001
SUBJECT:

Look. I'm finishing in about ten minutes. Are you okay? You've been really funny all day – and not funny ha ha like normal. I can hang around til five, if you like – go for coffee? We can go to the one by the station, not Starbucks. It's cheaper and they let you smoke. You up for that?

⊠

FROM: Martin Davies
TO: Safina Aziz
SENT: 16:21, Tuesday September 11, 2001
SUBJECT: RE:

Don't worry. I'll be fine.

⊠

FROM: Dan Jones
(mailto: dan@mcpl-media.co.uk)
TO: martin.davies@quantumfinance.co.uk
SENT: 16:22, Tuesday September 11, 2001
SUBJECT:

Intimacy. That's the word I was looking for. Intimacy. It's not the INTIMACY I miss. There you go, I knew I'd remember it eventually.

⊠

FROM: Susan Meredith
TO: Andrews, Darren; Aziz, Safina; Charles,
           Katherine; Davies, Martin; Gough, Lisa;
           Robinson, Suzie; Williamson, Joanne
SENT: 16:25, Tuesday September 11, 2001
SUBJECT: Tomorrow morning

Could those of you who are starting at 8.30 tomorrow morning please remember to start on the 556 queue, not the 558, as Expofax have advised us that the 558 connection is out of date and no longer reliable.

✉

FROM: martin.davies@quantumfinance.co.uk
TO:
SAVED: 16:26, Tuesday September 11, 2001
SUBJECT: RE: Tomorrow morning

Sue,

I will not be coming to work tomorrow because SHITCUNTFUCKBOLLOCKSFUCKSHITFUCKSHIT-FUCKSHIT

SAVED IN 'DRAFTS'

✉

FROM: martin.davies@quantumfinance.co.uk
TO:
SAVED: 16:27, Tuesday September 11, 2001
SUBJECT: RE: Tomorrow morning

Sue,

Unfortunately I will not be able to attend work tomorrow

SAVED IN 'DRAFTS'

✉

FROM: martin.davies@quantumfinance.co.uk
TO:
SAVED: 16:27, Tuesday September 11, 2001
SUBJECT: RE: Tomorrow morning

Hi Sue!

I regret to inform you that I will unfortunately be unable
to attend work tomorrow, or ever again for that matter,
as I am planning to kill myself. What am I talking about?
Even if I die and go to Hell I'll be right back here in the
morning.

SAVED IN 'DRAFTS'

✉

FROM: martin.davies@quantumfinance.co.uk
TO:
SAVED: 16:28, Tuesday September 11, 2001
SUBJECT: RE: Tomorrow morning

Sue

There are planes crashing into America

SAVED IN 'DRAFTS'

✉

FROM: Safina Aziz
TO: Martin Davies
SENT: 16:30, Tuesday September 11, 2001
SUBJECT: Home Time

Okay, well I'm going home now. If you need to talk about anything, call me.

✉

FROM: Martin Davies
TO: Safina Aziz
SENT: 16:34, Tuesday September 11, 2001
SUBJECT: RE: Home Time

You've probably gone home now. That doesn't matter. I think I'm about to fuck everything up.
   I'm just so bored with everything.
   I thought I loved you, but I look at the word now and it's alien, like a word somebody made up as a joke.
   None of this is making any sense. I'm sorry.

✉

FROM: Lloyd Thomas
(mailto:lloydt@callotech.co.uk)
TO: martin.davies@quantumfinance.co.uk
SENT: 16:37, Tuesday September 11, 2001
SUBJECT:

Emergency services in New York have found an Essex girl in the wreckage from the Twin Towers.

She appeared to have cuts and bruises, and when they asked her "Where are you bleeding from?" she replied, "Romford, you c**ts."

Don't tell me you're not smiling.

⊠

FROM: System Administrator
TO: Martin Davies
SENT: 16:40, Tuesday September 11, 2001
SUBJECT: Email Misuse

The following email has been blocked due to its content.

TO: SAFINA AZIZ
SUBJECT: RE: Home Time

You should be aware of the very strict company policy regarding email misuse. This issue will be forwarded to your department manager.

⊠

127

FROM: Martin Davies
(mailto: martin.davies@quantumfinance.co.uk)
TO: lloyd@callotech.co.uk
SAVED: 16:46, Tuesday September 11, 2001
SUBJECT: RE:

I'm not smiling.

✉

FROM: Martin Davies
(mailto: martin.davies@quantumfinance.co.uk)
TO: God
SENT: 16:48, Tuesday September 11, 2001
SUBJECT: Why?

Please get me out of here. I'm so fucking scared.

✉

FROM: Lloyd Thomas
(mailto: lloydt@callotech.co.uk)
TO: martin.davies@quantumfinance.co.uk
SENT: 16:52, Tuesday September 11, 2001
SUBJECT:

Okay, I've tried to say sorry for whatever it is I'm meant to have done, but I figure f**k you.

What do you f**king want, Mart? A f**king medal? A f**king shoulder to cry on? A f**king prize? You think you're alone in the f**king world? You think you're the only one who's f**king miserable? Everyone's f**king miserable, Mart.

Everyone.

✉

FROM: System Administrator
TO: Martin Davies
SENT: 16:55, Tuesday September 11, 2001
SUBJECT: Message Unsent

The following message did not reach its intended recipient:

        TO: GOD
        SUBJECT: WHY?

The recipient address was unknown.

✉

FROM: Martin Davies
(mailto: martin.davies@quantumfinance.co.uk)
TO: lloydt@callotech.co.uk; l.cullis@porter-simpsonporter.co.uk; Greenwood, Philip; McKenzie, Graham; Meredith, Susan; Cuccinello, Tony; Andrews, Darren; Aziz, Safina; Charles, Katherine; Davies, Martin; Gough, Lisa; Robinson, Suzie; Williamson, Joanne; Mayhew, Gini; Baker, Jenni; tobester69@hotmail.com; mhurley@jamstar.com; dan@mcpl-media.co.uk; friggyjo@yahoo.com; randystyle@bringme.co.uk; quangvp@hotmail.com; jizlober@fuckyou.co.uk; rowleyoda@inorbit.com; bootifulstu@buzzmail.com; benjster@hemail.com;
SENT: 17:00, Tuesday September 11, 2001
SUBJECT: 'Fucking Tuesdays'.

This is my life.

Maybe I read too many books on 'How To Write A Script'. Convinced myself that every story must have a beginning, a middle and an end, and that every protagonist must have a conscious desire.

There's no beginning and no middle. Everything is just a protracted last act, and any conscious desires I had have been battered and fucked up beyond all recognition.

To go back to a point when I was even remotely likeable or interesting would mean starting from scratch. I'd have to scrunch up every page or highlight every line and hit 'delete'.

What do I want? I want a good night's sleep. I want to wake up and know tomorrow will be better than today. I want the happy ending I've seen in all those sitcoms and adverts.

I haven't seen the TV today, but it sounds as if the world's ending, crashing into a chasm of our making. Times like this make clear the order of things, and if civilisation is about to dismantle itself backwards, we're the first ones lined up for extinction. Why do you think those planes flew into office buildings?

We are a disposable generation. Centuries of evolution and enlightenment thrown away in an orgy of shopping and recreational sex, and it only ever got us as far as the end of this sentence. We never saw this coming. You never saw this coming.

You might be reading this out of pity. You might be reading this out of morbid curiosity. You might be reading this because it's been forwarded to you as a joke. You might not be reading this at all. Either way, you know what happens next.

Have a nice fucking day.

✉

About the author

David Llewellyn was born in 1978. He grew up in Pontypool and graduated from Dartington College of Arts in 2000. He now lives in Cardiff.

David Llewellyn has had short stories published online, and has written comedy sketches for the BBC. He collaborated on a feature-length film script, 'Somewhere', performed live at the Cardiff Screen Festival in 2003.

Eleven is his first novel.

The Land as Viewed from the Sea
Richard Collins

Shortlisted for the Whitbread First Novel Award 2004, *The Land as Viewed from the Sea* is a beautifully-wrought, dream-like meditation on land, sea and the illusory nature of love.

Two friends work together on a smallholding: one allows the other to read the novel he is writing, *The Land as Viewed from the Sea*. As the novel unfolds, fiction begins to intrude upon reality, redefining the friends' relationship, and threatening to change their lives forever.

With great delicacy and intelligence, Richard Collins has written a love story which is at once innovative, timeless and deeply affecting.

"A compelling read, dreamlike and lifelike at the same time."
The Guardian

"An evocative story of dislocation and loss."
The Daily Telegraph

"Fresh, surprising and ambitious, Richard Collins' dark-hearted love story unfolds with immense narrative skill."
Whitbread Awards panel

ISBN 1-85411-367-4   £6.99

www.seren-books.com

Overland
Richard Collins

Home isn't a place on the map, it's a state of mind.

Sometime like 1978, somewhere like Europe, Oliver and Daniel are driving towards and away from home on a roadtrip to places that never were. Two men with very different purposes and meanings to their lives, travelling, for a while in the same direction.

Richard Collins' new novel is as vivid and atmospheric as his first, his prose both lucid and evocative. *Overland* is an exhilarating, comic, tender, crazy and ultimately moving account of two journeys towards love.

ISBN 1-85411-420-4   £7.99

Mr Vogel
Lloyd Jones

One day, a strange account of a lame man's mysterious quest is found in the attic of an antiquarian bookshop. The Vogel Papers, as they become known, lead our loveable guide on an epic ramble around his homeland, abetted by a motley troupe of drinking friends, academics, healers, writers and notorious eccentrics (not to mention a teddybear and a piglet or two), in search of a peculiar fellow called Mr Vogel. Funny, sad and warm-hearted, *Mr Vogel* is a celebration of the culture and landscape of one small country, and a reflection on the importance of hope.

Winner of the McKitterick Prize and shortlisted for the Bollinger Everyman Woodhouse Award.

"A rambling, redemptive mystery stuffed full of all things Welsh: rain, drink, wandering, longing, a preoccupation with death and the life that causes it. A bizarre and uncategorisable and therefore essential book."

Niall Griffiths

"One of the most dazzling books ever written about Wales."
Independent on Sunday

Lloyd Jones lives on the North Wales coast. After nearly dying of alcoholism and undergoing spells in hospital and living rough, he quit drinking and set off on a trip, on foot around Wales – a journey of more than a thousand miles, and the inspiration for this book.

ISBN 1-85411-380-1   £7.99

www.seren-books.com